What the Viewe...
Whistlejacket by Jo~~hn Hawkes~~

BOOKS BY JOHN HAWKES

NOVELS

Adventures in the Alaskan Skin Trade
The Beetle Leg
The Blood Oranges
The Cannibal
Death, Sleep & the Traveler
Innocence in Extremis
The Lime Twig
The Owl
The Passion Artist
Second Skin
Travesty
Virginie: Her Two Lives

PLAYS

The Innocent Party: Four Short Plays

COLLECTIONS

Humors of Blood & Skin: A John Hawkes Reader
Lunar Landscapes: Stories and Short Novels

WHISTLEJACKET

JOHN HAWKES

COLLIER BOOKS

MACMILLAN PUBLISHING COMPANY

NEW YORK

Copyright © 1988 by John Hawkes

Published by arrangement with Weidenfeld & Nicolson, New York, A Division of Wheatland Corporation.

Collier Books
Macmillan Publishing Company
866 Third Avenue, New York, NY 10022
Collier Macmillan Canada, Inc.

A portion of this novel appeared previously in *Conjunctions*.

Library of Congress Cataloging-in-Publication Data
Hawkes, John, 1925–
    Whistlejacket.
    I. Title.
PS3558.A82W48   1989   813'.54   88-34154
ISBN 0-02-043591-6

Cover photograph by Craig Dietz
Cover design by Darlene Barbaria

First Collier Books Edition 1989

10 9 8 7 6 5 4 3 2 1

PRINTED IN THE UNITED STATES OF AMERICA

FOR
SOPHIE

I

THE PHOTOGRAPHER

1

BEAUTY IS NOT in the eye of the beholder, as they say, but in the lens of the camera. The eye of the camera is the only eye that sees true beauty, which is to say the beauty of woman. Woman is a field of vision, woman is her own landscape. Through the thick, transparent lens of my camera—cameras I mean to say, but one will do for the metaphor—I see woman. Not women. Woman. Although I see both.

And given all this rhetoric, whose voice is this? Who am I? Only a twenty-eight-year-old fashion photographer. But I am also a horseman and fox hunter. A young man of the old school in a new life. And I love my work. I love horses. I love woman. Not women. Except perhaps for Virgie. But then she and I are sister and brother for all intents and purposes since I have been—or was until recently—her father's protégé from the time I was a boy of twelve. Virgie's mother, Alex, is a different matter. Alex is woman. Pure woman. And horsewoman. And now a widow. So I love Alex.

Whose voice is this? I don't know. And who am I? An innocent though not entirely pure photographer known as Mike to his friends and Michael to all the rest of them. Alex says I am everything she ever wanted in a young man and

3

she ought to know. Alex gives special stress to my nickname. Mike.

The third woman in the Van Fleet household is Barbara C. Buse, known only by her married name, Buse, which rhymes with "ruse." She alone remembers the summer afternoon when Virgie's father and my mentor decided that from then on she would be known as Buse. He thought she deserved to be addressed as a man and a man bearing her husband's family name at that. And also, he said, the name Buse, with its long *u* and hard *s*, brought such words and phrases to mind as "boost" in "boosting her up to mount a horse," though she never mounted with the aid of anyone in her life, or the *bustier*, that boned corselet best suited to a body as rich in flesh as hers. Besides, he said, the name made him think of "ooh!"—that word of the flappers—and so gave a little secret flip or fillip to the name. So Buse it was in speech and signature, though no one knew the how and why of it.

Except for myself. I came to know.

All photographic scenes that follow—scenes involving professional models—are arranged chronologically, from place to place, scene to scene, model to model, though the same model may appear and reappear in the photographic scenes. In time. There may be models who appear never to appear again in any scene and there may be more than one model—or professional woman of a certain kind in my business—in any given scene. Carol, Susan, Ashley, Sylvia, Bonnie are well named. For instance, Virgie and Alex and Buse could not have been models.

Adventures begin at home, she said. But little did I know what Alex meant. Home was not my word but hers, and little did I know the history or for that matter anything about the adventures, as she said, that occurred at Steepleton. No matter that the better part of my life—young, older—had been spent in many of the rooms she was thinking of whether she knew it or not.

* * *

The black and white corgi—long, pointed ears, face like a fox's, legs like a young pig's attached to the paws of a monstrous white rabbit—used to romp after Virgie and me when we were both young. "Corgi" is a word derived from the Welsh *cor*, which means dwarf, hence the name of that kind of stunted or dwarfed dog, for such is the breed now and was back then.

On the other hand, the horse called Captain turned out to be not just the sire but the mad sire as well of Alex's blooded mare, Lady Diana, or Lady Di as she is known, and such a horse means blood, hot, in heat, an aspect of Alex's nature I discovered only on my most recent visit to Steepleton.

Dog and horse must be related.

Animals. Female. And horse and woman and photographer's art are my loves. But against my will I came to detest the now long-dead corgi simply because Virgie fondled it whenever she could get her girlish hands on her mother's poor stunted animal. For years I pitied the nameless little beast and then came to loathe it and wanted to squat like Virgie and take it into my lap as Virgie did and play with it without mercy—and I do mean play—and then pull its great ears until it whimpered as it did at the hands of the little figure stooping down for a few moments in the dark of the stable. But I never laid hands on the corgi. For me the dog was a warning, just as were the spread skirts, the slippery riding pants, the giggles and quivering lips of Virgie. When Virgie turned all her youthful temperament in my direction, when she tried to make me aware of the touch of her hand and the feel of her narrow hips, then whether I pushed her on the swing or followed her into the stable, which was empty except for horses and perhaps a groom or two, it was then that I most disliked the little dog. How cruel it was to allow the corgi to follow us about, bobbing at the heels of pure desire. Virgie's desire and, despite what I say, my own.

* * *

"The trouble with you," Carol said, "is that you're too lucid."

It was an astute remark or at least interesting because impossible.

"I like that, Carol," I said. "But there's no such thing as too lucid. Lucid, yes, but not too lucid. Besides, if either of us is truly clear of mind and speech, it's you. Your lucidity is in your eyes. Why do you think you're here?"

My camera clicked. Silently my cameras, this one and then that one, registered the image, not the act, or registered the act and hence preserved the image. Two words essential to my life and art. Act and image.

She wiped her brow.

The only thing that interested me at the time was her name. Carol. I couldn't pronounce her family name. It was foreign. European. Only her given name interested me in the beginning, her name and her voice. Obviously I am speaking of the beginning.

First model. First scene.

One thing that can safely be said about me is this. I am not a Generic Stud. Or wasn't. I saw the two words in some newspaper or other or in a magazine or at least a text or a context that had nothing to do with me as photographer, biographer, person. Generic Stud, it said. Not me.

I am clean-shaven. My cheeks are as smooth as a baby's bottom, a phrase that suggests the names of two pipe tobaccos, Baby's Bottom and Barking Dog. The label on the can of the latter says that Barking Dog never bites. An old homily. But any dog will bite under the proper circumstances, just as any horse will kick.

Despite my penchant for technology, I do not shave with an electric razor. In my studio-loft, in the large space designed for the needs of the body—all of it from hair to nails, skin to teeth, defecation to the steam of the shower—there are three electric razors, all new, each a different make and model, all of them replaced randomly, whenever I find myself picking up a new razor. The interesting thing is that my electric shavers are all new but never used except, as occasion demands, by women. I myself prefer shaving in the traditional manner with beaver brush, British razor—head of soft bristles and handle of solid brass—and a thick soap mug that fits the hand and looks like a heavy cup or mug, and fits my grip as well as any of the electric razors. My shaving mug is made by Woods of Windsor, Traditional Perfumers since 1770, as the label says. An appealing date if we think of the American Revolution, but why bother? The point is me and my toiletry.

"Baby's Bottom . . ." I sometimes remark appreciatively when a naked woman and I happen to be using our razors or hot towels of a morning or night in my studio-loft. She is always naked. But inevitably I wear white boxer shorts. Imported.

Some dark secrets never come to light. Some riddles never submit to unraveling. Some mysteries remain unsolved. But not so the mystery of what occurred so recently at Steepleton. My lips, after all, are not sealed. Natural light and dark secrets are in the realm of innocence, the beat of a horse's hooves, the sounds of a silent photographer curling himself about his subject.

Remember?

"Lavatory," I said.
"Men's," Carol said.
"Right you are," I said, and off I went.

It was the first time that Carol and I lunched at this restaurant, The Flying Crane, which became our haunt for lunch from that moment on whenever our first lunch came to mind. It had a special place in our hearts since this first visit occurred not long after we met and began to work together. In some Japanese restaurants the facilities—odd word but somehow I acquired it—are still divided. Women. Men. Men. Women. Separate.

Modern fixtures. Black and white tiles. Bright light that appeared to have no source. A medicinal-looking wall dispenser half filled with liquid soap. But the soap was not medicinal. Not at all. I took my time and pumped the nozzle, between thumb and first finger rubbed together what I had collected in my palm, studied the stuff, lifted palm to nose, and sniffed. Unmistakable. That slippery. But perfumed. Perfume for Carol, though we were no more than acquaintances in the beginning of a professional collaboration.

Later amidst the tinkling and the sound of voices we did not hear, Carol rose and went off to *Women*. I waited, she returned, I dared to ask the question that no one except myself could ask. Could she possibly be expecting it?

She sat down. I asked my question.

"Is the soap the same in *Women* as it is in *Men*?"

"I don't know," she said, taking her card from her wallet and staring into my eyes with an expression that gave me no satisfaction. "I used the men's."

"Forced into it?" I asked.

"Oh, no, *Women* wasn't occupied. I just chose *Men*."

"Lucid," I said. "You see who's lucid."

"A little sweetener and we're all alike."

"Almost," I said.

We laughed, she paid the check, we left.

"Contact," said the voice on the phone.

"Good morning, Alice," I said. "Or is it night?"

"Contact" is our private code or rather hers for beginning a telephone conversation. As a verb "contact" means swing the propeller; as a noun someone of help to a speaker, dishonest or not. "Contact" is Alice's word for greeting, not mine, while "Alice" is our private code for what she and I call her when speaking together about an assignment, which means a place, an idea, a model. Alice is a woman who calls me about such matters. She offers me women. She asks me to take their photographs. We never speak of "shoot" or "a shoot." I think of Alice as the best of procuresses and I the purest man in the field whom she can telephone to do what she wants and what I for that matter want to do as well. Take their photographs. That's all. Or so it seems.

The real name of the person I nicknamed Alice is beside the point. The point is that Alice knows that her artificial name contains the Russian name of Alicia. She does not know that privately, to me only, Alicia refers to my friend Alexandra.

"It's morning," she said. "And you know it as well as I do, Mike."

"There are always people in sight."

"And people with cameras."

"Do you recognize those woods? Those shadows? That green field?"

"No. Do you?"

"Yes. Did anyone see me?"

"Not just anyone. Someone with a camera did."

"Was it you? Did you take my photograph?"

"No. But I saw you nonetheless."

2

THERE SHOULD HAVE been rooks. There should have been bells. Tones of mourning should have rung out from between the branches of high trees from towns and villages near and far to echo back in dull, unmistakable strokes our grief. But there was silence except for ordinary sounds.

It was 11:00 A.M. on a weekday in October. A clear day. The family cemetery. The Van Fleets' own. And where were the masses of mourners already gathered? No one besides ourselves? No one. I had expected half the town and all the Van Fleets' gathered friends and servants, relatives, those who had ridden with the deceased, sailed over the Van Fleet gates and hedges, ditches and fences, and chased the Van Fleet fox and drunk the stirrup cup under the eye of the deceased and admired his wife and horses and admired his daughter for her riding but not her beauty since she had none except perhaps in the shape of her body. Where were they all?

"Well," said Alex, "they're on time."

She was referring not to friends and relatives and neighbors but to the mortician's party and to the minister, a black and white figure waiting near the ready grave under the trees. The hearse gleamed in black contrast with earthen road, crisp, fallen leaves, its black planes and chromium trim and sheet of smoky glass reflecting back a man-made version and hence a travesty of what rooks and bells might have provided—appropriate evidence of finality and grief. Somber trappings.

Was our slow pace mere sham? Mere stroll through a tempered landscape toward old stones and angels that would never fly? Or was it mindless, unavoidable, the progress of all funeral parties that walk to the measured step of a bereaved widow or widower? Today my senses detected a violation of all that that burial scene demanded. There should have been mourners, lots of them, gathering to help Alex and Virgie and even me through the last rites, and surely they would have included those loyal retainers devoted to kennels and stables. But they were not there. And we alone could not provide the resounding silence to send him off and away—the Master of Foxhounds himself. My mentor. Hal or Handsome Hal but formally Harold O. Van Fleet, dead at a young age, all things considered. Sixty-two.

The four of us, pitiful number, advanced so slowly into the Van Fleet cemetery and toward the waiting grave and casket that I thought the living scene might cease altogether and become the still picture from which we'd never escape and in which the casket would never find its way from the straps that supported it to the bottom of the waiting grave.

Alex and myself, Buse and Virgie behind us. We were all there were to be. Since this was what Hal himself had insisted on, only Alex and Virgie and Buse and me when the time came, which it had. This Alex told me on our walk from the car to the site of the ordeal or privilege, however the shocking hour struck home.

"My dear Alex," said the minister, not at all intending to complete the sentence while from the drapery of his professional garb he extended pink hands.

"John," said Alex, acknowledging in the impoverished sound of his familiar name all the condolences he had to give. For the first time she took my arm in an unmistakable gesture; her true condolences would come from me.

"Why don't the four of you just gather around me in a semicircle?" the minister said, and I was aware that I was

standing directly in front of him with Alex on my left and
Virgie on my right and Buse a few steps behind me. Sur-
rounded by women and suddenly the central figure. Supported on either side by women, whereas Virgie and I
should have been supporting Alex, who should have been
the obviously bereaved of our party. But was she?

I flexed as if to move, her hand tightened on my left arm,
Virgie took hold of my right with stealth, with strength. The
great trees rose silently above us, the lichen-covered stones
of the long-dead Van Fleets leaned this way and that, and the
minister adjusted his purple stole and raised his prayer
book to read aloud.

Chapter and verse. Dear friends.

If I had held a camera as he was holding his prayer book,
and if I had raised it and begun to record the elements that
in their existence gave visual shape to utter absence,
through the viewfinder I would have seen the fluted sleeve,
white sail protruding from the stiff black cloth, a tip of his
white shoulder, the edge of the book as he turned in a
further effort to conceal what he was hiding, and then,
beyond him and briefly dappled, Harold's casket on its
straps, which were drawn tight by a steel mechanism hidden from sight, as was the pit beneath, by the usual folds of
thick green fabric that simulated grass. A photograph of this
moment would have been all the more faithful for being
obscured by those portions of the minister—sleeve, crook of
arm, sweep of skirt—that insisted on invading and then
using up the frame. I would have focused, I would have
caught my breath if I had seen one of the many photographs I might have taken, filling a glossy page not with the
expected grainy black and white but color.

I listened, I saw the brief curl of the minister's pink lip wet
in speech, the backs of the too-smooth hands holding the
small black book, the loud, even magisterial voice, and
beyond him the casket.

Harold's casket, though I could see a mere portion of it,
was large and heavy. Mahogany. Silver trim and handles.
Mahogany the dark wet color of a brown horse fresh from
the hunt field.

If I had had my lights, my cameras, I would have multiplied the dappling of sun and leaves, deadened some leaves and made others more white and green, would have layered like crystal the light that fell on the burnished casket and on the purple velvet cloth that covered the center portion. I would have carried the color from the minister's stole to the thick cloth on the casket, portrayed the dead man in the grip of his priest, and the purple I would have caught forever would have brought to the surface the dark and bloody red that makes the religious color possible.

But I had no camera. Thinking about cameras and photographs was inappropriate in these harsh circumstances. But for all that, I had my images and knew they could never fade.

Sniffing? Holding back tears? It was Buse, I realized, though it would have been unseemly to turn my head and look at her, Buse sniffing into a lady's cambric handkerchief. I listened, bemused and pleased, noting for the future, though I did not know why, that the only one of these three women to give way was Buse, who until that moment had been the least susceptible to displays of hurt, sentimental or not. Her heart, I had always thought, was as resilient as her hips were solid. Virgie was easily brought to tears or giggles, Alex to neither. I could count on Alex to experience strong emotions but keep them to herself. Wasn't it curious then that I doubted Alex's grief as for some reason I did, and knew without looking that Virgie's eyes were as dry as stones, though here was her father all but struck down dead at her feet?

Buse was wearing a burnt-brown knitted dress and a felt hat to match. Alex was dressed in gown and hat of a fresh, clear pond blue, one of the many shades of blue she wore when she was not wearing green for the sake of her auburn hair. Virgie wore black, the cropped hair was uncovered. I couldn't have dressed or posed them more effectively had they been models. Even down to the tall, pale young man in their midst. Slender young man, gray suit, white shirt, black oxfords, tie of many properly subdued colors. How different the picture would have been without me.

I saw that the rear door of the hearse was open, that a dark figure was sitting in the driver's seat, and that the great mound of earth removed from the grave was covered with sheets of the rough material intended to simulate green grass. Trickles of fresh earth appeared from beneath its edges just as wisps of auburn hair showed themselves from beneath the edges of Alex's hat.

The minister stopped reading. He waited. Then he explained why he was pouring a thin stream of ashes from a silver pocket vial into the shape of a small cross on the head of the casket. He recited two prayers, and prayers done and empty-handed, he stood once more facing us but to one side so that we had at last a full view of the casket.

We felt not the slightest motion in the air around us. Minister and nature conspiring. In minutes he would remove the purple cloth from the casket and the lowering of the casket would be accomplished. When we were gone. It had been agreed that we would not wait for the burial itself. But we would know that the ashen cross would be carried safely to its place in the bottom of the grave and lie intact until the first shovelfuls of fresh earth struck the lid of Hal's casket.

With a glance from the minister Alex stirred, gave me to feel her intentions through the hand on my arm, turned us around somehow, and, while the minister watched, led our party back along the dirt road. I stumbled, I smelled Alex's perfume, a church bell, tuned to the freshness of a morning in early autumn, sounded. Grief at last acknowledging the death of Hal.

When we reached the car and I held the door for Buse, I noticed what I had not seen when we had started out—a saddle. On the floor of the back seat. I watched Buse leaning down to enter the car without grace or any awareness of me. She slid across the seat, the edges of her caramel-colored skirt rose on her beige stockings. She twisted her large legs to avoid the saddle, which someone had not bothered to heave into the trunk. I recognized it—one of the German jumping saddles that had belonged to Hal. One stirrup iron showed, the other was concealed beneath the bulk of leather.

One broad saddle flap, polished from use, was bent in a bow. There it was, still partly on its nose where it had fallen, a big thing filling the space into which Buse was trying to fit her feet. Buse looked like a big woman some lesser photographer would like to shoot, as they say, sitting as she was on the edge of the rear seat of a handsome car, hips swung to the side, knees raised, skirt raised, accommodating herself as best she could to the saddle but clearly distracted by something or someone else. Click.

Virgie was not much larger than a jockey so that Buse needn't have tried so hard to make room. There was plenty of room for Virgie, who had already dipped into the car and was leaning her head back into the gray upholstery, eyes closed, white hands folded with more than resolution in her lap. Small lap, black dress, small white hands with the rough square-ended fingers of the born rider, gender notwithstanding. She wore no makeup, no fingernail polish, the ends of her fingers were square, everything about her was weathered and girlish both.

"Before lunch," she said suddenly, "I'm going to take a shower."

From the front seat I allowed myself to twist and look once more at Buse. It occurred to me that when a woman reveals her body unwittingly—I was studying the dress pulled askew, the sheer size of one of her knees—then the fact that no one, especially a man, is intended to see what her clothes and posture accidentally reveal increases disproportionately the drama that at the moment is causing the woman's evident distraction. Large leg. Intimacy. Hal's saddle. I looked back at the macadam road.

There are those who want to see, those who never think of it. There are those who want to be seen, those who don't. And those who do not wish to be seen fall into three categories: those who have no idea that anyone would bother to look at them, those who hide from being seen or watched, and finally those who know that anyone who looks at them once will look again. The plain, the shy, the furtive. Which will you have? Of those who wish to be seen we find the exhibitionist, the vainglorious, the seductive. A harder choice.

As for myself I want to see. I am a carnivorous watcher and I pursue them all. No one of them is uninteresting, no matter how much or little our subjects—for all of them are subjects, which is not the same as models—may think of themselves. But for me the pursuit quickens when I find myself among those who do not wish to be seen. They are the ones I most want to see.

3

GRANDFATHER VAN FLEET became a source of embarrassment and then genuine worry to his son and daughter-in-law. But the more the old man deteriorated, the more delight he provided for the Van Fleet children, especially for Michael, who was not a legitimate member of the family. Grandfather's only child, a son, and his daughter-in-law did the best they could to preserve the old man's life and reputation, to ensure his safety, and to prevent him from bringing to total ruin the family name, while the children—Michael and Virgie and Toots—watched and listened, tittered and giggled, crept down the stairs late at night when Grandfather was carried home, and, best of pleasures, invaded the old man's private apartment when the young maids were attempting to give him a bath.

Grandfather was short and wiry. He was immaculate in his mind and person until he failed. He wore a pince-nez and tailor-made suits, tiny black shoes and flowering silk ties, a black bowler, and topcoats cut to his trim little figure and of weight and color to match the season. He was esteemed, his reputation was unassailable, in his time he was known throughout the state as the only man to be trusted when it came to horses, racing, and fox hunting as well. The races could not go on without him, his were the knowledge and authority on which everyone depended. He had an uncanny eye for dishonesty and more than once had strolled among trembling horses mere minutes before the field was to go to the gates and stopped, requested in his mild voice that this horse or that be hosed down in his presence, and had watched with trainer, jockey, owner, stableboy, whoever could get close enough to see, as under the jet of water a big black revealed himself to be a bay, or a dark brown filly became pure white. Walter T. Van Fleet could always detect the real horse beneath the false color, or the drugged horse from that same animal in its natural state.

Grandfather lived in his own apartment in his son's home. Steepleton was a vast arrangement of bricks and gables, wings and chimneys that from the distance looked like the Pipes of Pan—the chimneys, that is—a mansion severe or serene depending on the light and the mood of the surrounding oaks, and constructed solely, it seemed, to house Grandfather's apartment, Grandfather's life-sized portrait of Whistlejacket and his daughter-in-law's fortepiano, both of which dominated the main salon. The several rooms devoted to Grandfather's personal life, the original George Stubbs oil painting of the great horse towering in the evening light on his hind legs, the fortepiano built especially for the gifted wife of the old man's son and only child—these, it seemed, had determined from the start the reason for Steepleton's existence, had guided the first ancestor's eye, the architect's hand, when Steepleton was first conceived and ground broken.

Grandfather insisted on having a key to his apartment and until the trouble started was careful to use it when he went off by chauffeured car and train to his professional days among horses and devotees of racing and hunting. In fact, he locked his rooms specifically against the children, though he smiled at them when he returned at dusk and when they were gathered at the long table or whenever he came down to attend with the rest of the family one of his daughter-in-law's evening solo recitals on the fortepiano. But his rooms had to undergo daily cleaning—his daughter-in-law insisted that his apartment be set to rights like the rest of Steepleton—and what two young women in white uniforms could control three teasing, energetic children and still manage to clean and sweep, fling up the windows, make up the high little old-fashioned bed, and scrub the old-fashioned porcelain tub? It was a hopeless task, and so the children had their run of Grandfather's apartment, were familiar with all Grandfather thought to be private and beyond the inquisitive touch and sight and prying of the children even before the trouble started. The children darted in and out of the rooms expressly forbidden to them when the door at the end of the long hallway was ajar and the bedclothes were stuffed into the open windows. With sudden reverence or flashes of fear in the aura of Grandfather's old age they sat in the old man's leather chair, studied the watercolor portraits of famous horses hung around the walls of that first room; in the second room, the bedroom, they pulled up the skirts of the little mahogany bed and tried to see beneath it until the younger of the girls in white shouted and chased them away from one of Grandfather's best secrets. Even more alluring was the bathroom with its black and white tiles and porcelain sink and tub. It was evident that Grandfather enjoyed smoking in his bathroom, and here and there on the white curves of the fixtures were the golden stains of long-dead cigars.

The trouble started when Grandfather began arriving at Steepleton late for the evening meal. Aunt Alexandra, as Michael called her, was a forbearing woman, yet night after night her frown grew more pronounced and her voice more saddened as she glanced at her husband and once again delayed the serving of the roast of beef or pair of ducks or of whatever sat on the cook's platter.

"Oh, well, Alex," Uncle Harold would say, "I guess we had better go ahead without him." With these words the car would inevitably arrive in the driveway and inevitably Will, the combination butler-chauffeur, would help Grandfather into the house and up to his apartment and finally back down to his place at the head of the table, where the rest of the uneasy diners waited.

"Drink," the children overheard Uncle Harold murmur to his wife one late evening after Grandfather had been unusually late to dinner and unusually silent and unsteady at the table. "My father is beginning to drink."

"I thought so," said Aunt Alexandra. "Can you do anything, Hal?"

"No," said Uncle Harold. "Will reports that he's drinking at least a bottle of vodka a day just in his rooms. Lord knows what he's drinking at the clubs. Will showed me the bottles stacked up in cartons out in the barn. Will's his accomplice. He just couldn't get out of it."

"To think that he could fool us all this long," said Aunt Alexandra. "And he's such an old man to change his life so completely."

"Drinking himself to death," said Uncle Harold. "That's what it is."

So Grandfather grew increasingly late for meals and increasingly unsteady and slow in his movements. He began forgetting things, his furled umbrella, his cane, his gray suede gloves, and then occasionally his wallet. More and more he failed to meet Will at the station and was driven back to Steepleton by strangers. If he spoke at all, which was rarely, he limited his few slurred words to his daughter-in-law, whose warm coppery hair and complexion naturally pink and white the old man had always admired. He spilled his food at the table, staining his tie, his shirtfront, his large starched cuffs, the tablecloth. He refused to give up his empty vodka bottles but kept them himself until he had collected cartonfuls, which he was finally forced to leave outside his door for Will late in the night.

Aunt Alexandra was concerned about the demoralizing effect the poor old man was surely having on the children. Of course, she could not know that the opposite was true, that the children were thriving on Grandfather's antics and were pursuing him now with new relentlessness. There was a light in their eyes as bright and significant as the new light that shone in Grandfather's bloodshot eyes. Grandfather was becoming crafty and so were the children.

Then the telephone calls began from this police station or that as Grandfather was discovered in this city or that one, happily wandering unfamiliar streets—disheveled, self-soiled, doubly pleased that he was freely traveling those midnight streets without a single shred of identity about his person. Walter T. Van Fleet no longer knew that he was Walter T. Van Fleet.

"My father doesn't know who he is," said Uncle Harold more than once to Aunt Alexandra, "and yet he's recognized in every gin mill within a hundred miles."

"It's depressing," Aunt Alexandra would say. "We really can't go on like this."

"No," Uncle Harold would say, "we can't."

And then the telephone would ring and Uncle Harold would dress himself in custom-tailored suit and tie and drive off in search of Grandfather.

Embarrassment had given way to genuine worry. But there was more to come. Days and nights when it seemed that Grandfather had disappeared for good, days and nights when the strain left dark shadows on Uncle Harold's long, narrow face, when Aunt Alexandra tried unsuccessfully to comfort her husband, when often dinner was not served at all. It was in this period that the children were most alert, or so they thought, and managed, all three, to awaken each other in order to spy on what were now Grandfather's infrequent returns to Steepleton and his predawn baths.

There was the sound of the car, the never-failing presence of Will in his cap and nightshirt and trousers, Aunt Alexandra wearing her deep rose-colored robe and holding wide the front door, and then the staggering, and Grandfather's energetic shout as Will and Uncle Harold carried the limp, disheveled man up the stairs, the rousing out of the two young maids, who accepted charge of Grandfather and, amidst his sudden cries of greeting, proceeded to administer the predawn bath.

After Will had garaged the car, after the adults were quiet—Will once more in bed with his wife, the cook, in their room above the kitchen, Aunt Alexandra and Uncle Harold settled in their adjoining apartments, all of Steepleton sunk once more into the final remaining hours of sleep—it was then that Grandfather's safe return was celebrated.

Steam, great cakes of scented soap, two large brownish yellow sponges that belonged as much in the stable as in

21

Grandfather's tiled bathroom, Grandfather still on his feet and tottering fully clothed and as best he could beside the filling tub while the two young women, wearing only clumsily donned white uniforms, their black hair undone and their faces puffy with interrupted sleep, steadied Grandfather and leaned over the noisily filling old porcelain tub—thus began the ritual in which Grandfather momentarily regained his memory, his strength, the scrubbed condition appropriate to the oldest living and most esteemed Van Fleet.

Each time that Grandfather was subjected to the scalding water, the soaping, the sponging, the struggle with the two young maids, each time that the maids lent their youth to Grandfather's age, he recovered more completely and for a longer time. Each bath began more violently than the last and ended with a longer-lasting calm. The filling tub roared and pounded like a ship's engine, the steam billowed and curled from the large, high-ceilinged bathroom into the waiting bedroom, where Michael was always the only child to see Grandfather safely to bed. "You bitches!" the old man shouted as a shriveled arm or spindly leg appeared through the tumult of splashing water and rolling steam. "You she-devils!" The old man's soiled clothing sailed forth, fell to the sopping wet floor; the young women pushed and shoved Grandfather in pretended anger, undressed him rudely, laughing all the while like the strong young girls they were. Grandfather resisted, fought back, pulled with little purple hands on the white half-open dresses that buttoned from throat to hem—or unbuttoned—and served as the maids' uniforms, so that occasionally, long after Toots had carried the hapless Virgie off to bed, Michael caught glimpses of their large gleaming legs or forearms smooth and strong. Grandfather splashed the maids, the smell of tobacco smoke came through the steam—Grandfather was smoking his pipe in his bath!—there were plunging sounds, brief glimpses of a half-bared bosom that caused Michael to blush and frown. Then out of the blurred and misty bathroom poured sudden silence, a strange long gagging sound, sudden suppressed giggles, a long cry caught, it seemed, in Grandfather's wind-pipe, and suppression, peace. The two young maids were subdued, respectful when at last they lifted Grandfather from the tub and dressed him in his lilac silk pajamas and propped him, limp and smiling, on three plump pillows high on his narrow bed between fresh white sheets.

Grandfather miraculously recovered. He was allowed out of his apartment. He gained strength, he parted his thin black hair in the middle as before, brushed it with his two silver brushes, began to groom himself. He spoke, he had a kind word even for the children. His last quarter of a bottle of vodka remained untouched. He behaved himself at Aunt Alexandra's table. His eyes cleared, he expressed a keen wish to join the hunt, which occasionally he did to Aunt Alexandra's alarm and Uncle Harold's pride. But Grandfather did not fall, did not disgrace himself.

No one could account for the change. No one except Michael and the two maids saw the remnant of fierce light that still lurked in the corners of the old man's eyes, and only the maids understood its significance. Grandfather was thinking, devising a scheme. He knew exactly what he wanted during his last weeks or months of life and was earning his liberty, earning trust, until he could swiftly satisfy his scheme before losing his rational mind altogether.

In this final period of incubation Grandfather was as serious and obedient and lucid as anyone could wish. He helped to redesign and expand the kennels, he encouraged Aunt Alexandra to resume her family recitals on the forte-piano. He was civil to the two young maids but acted as though he had no recollection of the bathing episodes they had shared. Once more he was Walter T. Van Fleet, once more he undertook his responsibilities in the various worlds of competition horses. He was the champion of integrity, a man whose professional memory and judgment could be trusted.

And then the inexplicable recovery inexplicably collapsed. There were no telephone calls, no respectable strangers, not even cartons of empty bottles in the hallway. One morning Grandfather set off on his business, his little shoulders tight in a gray topcoat, little black shoes polished by Will, black bowler atop his head like a cork in a bottle, and returned that evening as usual. Except that he was with a woman.

There was nothing gaudy about the first woman Grand-father brought home to Steepleton. She was not unduly young, her clothes suggested modesty. Yet everything about that woman betrayed her body. From the way she stood and swayed and with one hand clutched Grandfather's arm and with the other gripped his little bowler hat, it was evident that her nakedness could never be concealed, that hers was a nakedness always exposed no matter how she tried to dress herself. In they came, letting the majestic front door of Stee-pleton swing wide. They entered in the midst of their mutual laughter. Grandfather made no explanations, he did not try to introduce his friend—simply because Grandfather had forgotten the woman's name and his own as well.

Late the following morning they left and late the following night Grandfather returned, but again not alone. The second woman he brought home to Steepleton was quite different from the first, a small, plump person as young as the youn-ger of the two maids who had given Grandfather such devoted care, a stockingless girl wearing a skirt that reached hardly below her hips, and obviously quite drunk, as Uncle Harold said, upon arrival. Grandfather mustered all the dignity he had, looked straight ahead, puffed out his chest, lifted his chin, and slowly escorted his second guest up the broad stairway and out of sight.

The children marveled at Grandfather's courage, Aunt Alexandra made no attempt to hide her puzzlement and dismay, the two maids grew sullen, Uncle Harold found his father's final antics amusing until without warning he put an end to the happiest of Grandfather's days. The shaming of the family, the ruining of the family name, lasted through a total of five women. While it did last, before Uncle Harold intervened, Grandfather grew increasingly unshaven, un-washed, unsightly. His little person was consumed in his pursuit of passion. His fierce eyes were sightless in the old man's determination, his crooked smile was set. He could not talk, would not have appeared in public fully clothed had not each of his willing women done her best to dress him. Michael overheard Uncle Harold telling Aunt Alex-andra that apparently each of the women helped the old man onward to the next. No man, said Uncle Harold, had even come so close to total satiety. It took its toll.

When it ended, when Grandfather was confined for the second and final time to his apartment, when he was denied any access to that inexhaustible supply of women large or small, young or middle-aged that existed beyond Steepleton, when it was over, the stillness that settled over Steepleton was not the relief of peace and normalcy but the silence of some invisible disease.

Grandfather was put to bed. His drapes were drawn. Drained of desire, the old man was drained of life. His skin became like soft white tissue, his beautiful semblance of a wolf's grin was only silly. His diet was reduced to soup, tea, toast, and soft-boiled eggs fed to him by the younger of the now-grieving maids. Grandfather's scheme could not have been a greater success, a greater failure.

Only one consolation remained for Michael, who did not give up his habit of entering Grandfather's apartment every night while the rest of Steepleton slept on and of staring at Grandfather from the old man's bedroom door. It was this—that the younger of the two maids was also faithful to the little man in the ruin, the silence, the helplessness, the progressive fading and disintegration of the scrap of silk that was Walter T. Van Fleet's old age.

Fighting! Struggling! At one o'clock in the morning and in total silence Grandfather and the younger maid were fighting!

It was not at all what Michael had ever expected to discover upon arriving at the old man's bedroom door. How could it be? What had come over Grandfather? How had he managed to get out of bed? Where had he found the last surge of strength to leap from his bed—everything about the darkened scene suggested to Michael that the old man had done just that, leapt from his bed—when Michael knew as well as anyone that the old man was dying, daily and nightly and hourly. Propped into a half-sitting position on the pillows as plump and white as the geese that now and then came up from the pond as if to attack the house, with his little hands and brittle arms placed properly in waiting position on the tightly stretched white sheets and rose-colored blankets, obviously Grandfather was dying. Everyone knew what only Grandfather himself and Virgie did not. That he was dying.

But the bedclothes were awry! Grandfather was standing on his little feet like a boxer, his eyes were open!

It was a furious surprising scene that Michael in his robe and pajamas had come upon. It was all the more frightening because of the silence. Surely Grandfather might have shouted as he used to shout in the bathroom? Surely the girl might have called for help? Who would hear them? Who at that dark hour would come to hinder Grandfather and help the maid?

Did she need help?

The room was dark, it hardly smelled any longer of cigar and pipe smoke and of the deepest brown tobacco—brown the rich black color of horses that are called brown—as once it had when Grandfather smoked in bed, lighting his pipes or long cigars with wooden matches. The windows were shut for fear of drafts, the only light came from a small bedside lamp whose dark coral-colored shade had been knocked a firm blow so that a single funnel of light was cast across the rumpled bedcovers, which Grandfather's faintly breathing body had barely warmed. But there he was in deep shadows wrestling with the big girl who for so many nights had sat beside him, her black hair down and shining with natural oils, her hands folded in her lap, her strength transformed into patience that made her younger than her sturdy, resilient age of twenty.

In the silence Grandfather hopped about, the girl fended him off. The shadows followed them, enfolded them, revealed them. Grandfather lunged. He caught her. His grin was wide. His eyes were bright, clear, determined, crafty. He lost her. She reached a hand across her chest, attempted to pull up the shoulder of the bright green robe and cheap, pale nightdress beneath. But they were torn! She was taller than Grandfather, heavier, stronger—or had been—and yet he had snatched at her nightclothes, torn them down!

Later, when Michael lay breathing heavily in his own bed in the dark, he had no recollection of deciding to intervene, no idea how he had left the doorway to Grandfather's bedroom and plunged into the shadows and joined the wrestlers, held the old man tight so as to free the girl. But so it had been and his first shame was that Grandfather had fought back. For a moment the old man had not moved at all, and then had erupted, had twisted around and peered at his captor with recognition, without belief, surprise and anger wrinkling still more the old man's face, and, baffled as ever, had suddenly tried to jerk away, had bucked, lurched to the side, had tried to throw off this stranger who had dared to interfere in the personal life of Walter T. Van Fleet. That was the shame, that for some reason he had not expected Grandfather to be so strong or to resist him with such vehemence. It had taken all his strength to remain on his feet, horrified that Grandfather was fighting back. His second shame was worse, was nothing less than humiliation.

Around Grandfather's thrashing head he caught sight of the girl's face clear and unmoving in the blasts of thunder and lightning, wind and rain set off by Grandfather, whom he might not be able to restrain an instant more. The girl's dark hair floated in the shadows and darkness around her. She was looking at him, not with relief—not at all—not with any girlish smile of gratitude. Nor was she making any move to help him, when in an instant Grandfather might break away and attack a mere boy of twelve as he had attacked this hefty girl. And Grandfather, whenever his face came into view, was not smiling as he had been throughout the girl's ordeal. Quite the opposite. Grandfather was grimacing! Grimacing! At a mere boy whose weight was even less than the old man's and who had only meant to help and who, of all those living in Steepleton and even though he was not a Van Fleet, probably loved Grandfather the most. But the expression on the hovering handsome face of the girl had changed from surprise and disbelief—she must have wondered where Michael had come from, why Michael was up at such an hour and suddenly attempting to subdue his adopted grandfather—had changed from surprise and disbelief to anger. That was it, the younger of the two maids was angry at him, displeased, when he had expected only the opposite. His face grew hot, and it was not Grandfather who was wet with perspiration but himself.

It was a dreadful situation, a time of the purest humiliation. But just when he thought he could not last a moment longer and when he felt Grandfather breaking loose, snapping his bonds—and who could survive the old man's fury? surely not Michael—the old man suddenly went limp, sagged in his arms. The girl leapt forward, spots and curves of bareness visible in the shifting of her torn garments, and caught Grandfather, took him into her own sweet-smelling arms, returned him carefully to the bed. For days and weeks longer he remained with empty face and feathery breath and then, one morning, without the slightest sign of struggle, he died.

For now the girl was bending over the bed, tucking up the covers, settling Grandfather's arms atop the covers. Across from her Michael was waiting, head down, breath returning, hair damp. The humiliation would be even worse, he knew, in the darkness of his own room. At last the girl straightened, he raised his head. She looked at him.

"You silly boy," she said, and he was trying his best to meet her eyes, "you should not have done that."

But what had he done? And was she really angry with him when the horrible episode was over?

In the interim, which was both long and short, between Michael's struggle with Grandfather and the old man's death, Michael developed an ailment in his chest, something between a mild infection and that turbulent inflammation that lives half in the imagination, half in the lungs, which exactly suited Toots Van Fleet. Michael's ailment was accompanied by a brief return of childhood asthma, worst at night, when it was both feared and relished by its young sufferer. The nature of Michael's complaint was of no interest to Toots. She cared only that it existed, that it was evident, and so meant that Michael, the only boy living at Steepleton, was dressed in the late afternoon as he was at night. It was essential for Toots, a secretive girl rapidly maturing in ways the most observant parent could not have imagined, that Michael's ailment not be severe enough to confine him to bed or to quarantine him away from the others—namely, herself and the little confused camp follower, Virgie. And this ailment of Michael's was not.

The point was pajamas. A slight respiratory infection or common head cold, if not considered unduly contagious, allowed the victim to be up and around in his pajamas at a time of day when no suspicion adhered to such a form of dress in a child—except in the mind of Toots herself. So Michael wore his pajamas among the girls, as their kindly, nurturing mother called them, when the late afternoon hung fading from the window ledges, when faint darkness stole into the rooms upstairs and down, when no electric lights were as yet switched on. The end of the day, the start of night, when adults were not predisposed to give a thought to children.

It was nothing for the sisters to wear their polka-dotted pajamas in the late afternoon whether sick or not. Pajamas, even without robes, were appropriate enough for girls. Some might have said that Toots at fifteen was too old to lounge in her room or Virgie's, drinking tea and playing with the buttons of her pajama jacket or sometimes Virgie's, then using the round of a small satin pillow toward some intrusion upon Virgie's person that required in the older girl a distracted smile, a violent quivering of the thin arms, a showing of her two overly large white front teeth that corresponded to her eyes wide open. But their well-meaning mother gave Toots her head, a figure appropriate to horse lovers, and Toots did not appear to abuse the tea-and-lady's-magazines-in-pajama privileges. Given her head, Toots ran any way but straight.

One late afternoon, when Michael was trying to suppress his wheezing, easier for him to hear than others, and Grandfather lay in his last coma, which had all the appearances of peaceful sleep and which relieved the household yet constrained its freedom, Toots, with her skinny body and hands that shook, a girl whose only plumpness was in her lips, an asset which she made luminescent in purple red, frangipani red, pearl pink, silvery rose and then bit incessantly, invented a game. For a few hours poor little Virgie knew the ordinary child's excitement while Michael warily watched to see what Toots had in store for them. He was convinced that Toots, three years his senior, was too old to play games and was probably incapable of inventing such a complicated thing as a game. She liked mirrors, presumably in order to see her high cheekbones, long face, sunken eyes, high forehead, and, most of all, her typical Van Fleet lips, the fleshy double heart-shaped lips—the lower reflecting back the upper—of a mouth and jaw so narrow that she remembered still the days when she had been mocked as "Fish-mouth" or "Fish-lips," which no doubt accounted for her habit of biting her lips no matter how alluringly she did them. Toots at least found her own facial features attractive, she was vain, she appealed to hand mirrors in a way that frightened Michael yet lured him on. What did "Fish-lips" offer should a kiss occur?

Michael was wheezing only mildly on that day Toots first orchestrated the game. It was raining, it was a cold late afternoon, far from where Whistlejacket hung in the heart of Steepleton, up on the second floor and nearly to the end of the children's wing, as it was known, there Michael lay in his room, comfortably propped on pillows and comfortably wheezing. He listened to himself and to the rain, only his own ear was attuned to the sharp, unrhythmical notes struck faintly inside his chest. He was neither reading nor daydreaming but merely enjoying the hateful bronchial music in luxurious idleness. The light in the small room was of the dark amber shade of the last leaves hanging in the rain, leaves dropping now and then from the branches of the aged wet oak outside his window.

Toots arrived—had he been expecting her?—and summoned him to the girlishly decorated room that was reserved for overnight girl guests and was rarely occupied except by Toots and Virgie in the afternoons. Their own bedrooms were large with puffy beds and swirled dressing tables and stuffed chairs covered in shiny flowered chintz. But Toots and Virgie were not hospitable, even to each other, and preferred the little cozy room intended for a girlfriend who never came. The room contained two soft daybeds with coverlets and bolsters and a dressing table smaller than those of Toots and Virgie. The floor space, such as it was, was covered with a white long-haired rug longing for the bunny slippers worn by young girls or better still their bare feet. There was a long mirror on the closet door and in the closet itself a row of satin-wrapped hangers on which no dresses hung. The absence of the girlfriend who did not exist contributed an extra piquancy to this room that could lose its innocence in a word, a look, a widening of nostrils, a toss of the head.

Toots told Michael not to wear his robe. Dubiously, he left that beige garment—a present from Aunt Alexandra—on the foot of the bed and followed her. Toots was tall for her age, she wore only the two pieces—jacket and pants—of a set of boy's pajamas. Her thin blond hair, browning toward the crown of her head, lay close to the narrow shape of her skull and did not reach her shoulder blades because, as he knew, she had recently cut her hair with a pair of nail scissors. He attempted not to think of her buttocks.

When they arrived in the room where the promised tea and cakes were waiting—it was a room reached across a carpeted hallway and involved on either side a set of three steps—Michael began to wheeze with just enough volume so that he knew all of them must hear him. His forehead was wet. He was immediately embarrassed that his fly was never quite concealed by the front of his pajama jacket. Virgie sat curled up, waiting for them as she had to be. But who was the big person seated tentatively in the shadows of the guest room that afternoon? Could he bear to know?

The light was the color of the last dying leaves, the light was drenched with rain outside the window. And this brutal darkening color was suffused with the pink tones cast by one of the small lamps on the little dressing table. The room looked like a mock bedroom on display in a large department store—and into the allure of such impersonality he stepped, surprised and chagrined by the presence of none other than the large girl he had avoided since the night the two of them had met over the unhappily lively figure of Grandfather. It was she, Molly, too big a girl for this room. At least she looked as uncomfortable as he.

There was a good and obvious reason for her discomfort aside from the furtiveness she detected in this small gathering, aside from her age, aside from the fact that she did not know what Toots wanted her to do. The obvious reason was that in so many unspoken words the mother of these two unusual girls, Aunt Alexandra, in all other ways so generous and unsuspicious, had made it clear that she preferred Molly to keep her distance from the children. Avoid them is what she meant, though she could never have spoken such a word. Why was not clear. Alexandra preferred to play musical pieces that were not strident. She was soft, smiling, the raspberry or auburn color of her hair suggesting a motherly rather than fiery nature. She was not a woman to hurt the feelings of a local girl working at Steepleton.

But there it was. And Molly knew on that first afternoon that she should not have been sequestered alone with the children. Not for a moment. And Toots knew it and so, vaguely, did Michael. Nonetheless Toots had cajoled Molly into joining them. Disobedience. Violation. Taboo.

Toots told Michael to sit down. She gave an unconscious hitch to her pajama bottoms. The two white daybeds, one reluctantly occupied by the maid, were catercornered from each other against the white walls. Michael tried to sit on the edge of the empty daybed, but it was not as firm as its twin, was in fact soft, apparently contained no coils and springs, was nothing but the apparition of the piece of furniture it was intended to be. Down he sank. He was trapped. The bolsters slid down around him.

Virgie, whose little face Toots had savagely made up in oily colors that crudely simulated the faces of beautiful women in Toots's magazines, declared that she did not understand the game and was afraid. Molly began to rise, the rain hissed at the windows, Toots thrust upon Molly a cup of tea clattering and dancing on its white bone china saucer. Michael wiped a blue sleeve across his forehead. Then the cakes. Powdery flat cakes each bearing in its center a bright red eye. The cakes crumbled before they reached the mouth. Pieces and crumbs and considerable amounts of confectioners' sugar in the lap.

Molly brushed herself and again moved to rise. Toots,

barefooted and perspiring, stood in front of the still uncomfortable and puzzled girl and explained the game, which,
she said, wouldn't take long. Molly and Michael had only to
stay where they were. Toots and Virgie would leave the room
and wait twenty minutes and then return. Then Molly
would tell Toots what had happened during all the time
Molly and Michael were alone.

Molly thought for a moment and then said it would be
much better if Toots and Michael stayed alone in the room.
Molly wasn't needed at all and had work to do.

But Toots begged and raised her chin and shivered and
with a bare toe knocked over the empty teacup Molly had
set on the floor. Toots clasped her hands and struck and
broke a dramatic pose and in desperation whispered that it
wouldn't work unless Molly agreed to try it. Twenty minutes. That was all.

Molly laughed and said she had a better idea. Why didn't
Toots just go ahead and kiss Michael? Toots blushed, ran her
hands down her protruding hips, so bony that she never
wore shorts or a swimsuit in the summer, and caught a few
strands of yellow hair behind an ear. She glanced at herself
in the mirror on the dressing table. Then, biting her lips and
in a different, harder voice, she said that they were wasting
time.

Molly recognized that tone of voice.

Virgie tried and failed to resist her much older sister. Toots
yanked Virgie out of the little classic chair, the small girl's
voice squeaked and died, the other door to the room opened
and then closed. Closed. They were alone. Michael and the
girl who had an Irish body, as he had heard Uncle Harold tell
Aunt Alexandra one afternoon in jest. An Irish body.

His chest became as tight and porous as a stone on a
beach. Must she hear? And except for the sounds he was
making—golden bees warring with well-drilled hordes of
flies, the orchestra's triangle pinging according to the signals
of the conductor's arrogant baton, the sudden insurgence of
the silvery pipes of the cathedral's organ, the whole stony
edifice inside his chest beginning to shake—he could hear
only the silence in which something was going to happen,
according to Toots.

He heard a cough. She was smiling at him. She had kicked off her shoes, she had unfastened a few buttons top and bottom of the white dress that had shrunk in the laundry, she was leaning back slightly—no offering could have been larger!—and was bracing herself on either side with extended arms. A strap had gotten tangled, misplaced in the large opening at the top of the dress. She opened another button, reached inside, adjusted herself, but when she had settled back again, he could only see more.

He managed a faint drooping at the corners of his mouth. He could hardly breathe and certainly could not talk. But then, before he could consider licking his lips or looking at her again, he began the long self-justification which, even in silence, he thought the person on the other bed could hear, an argument that included the idea that since he was not a Van Fleet by blood, he must all the more behave with propriety, brush aside the childish enticements invented by Toots.

But wait! Was she, before his eyes and while still smiling as if she were doing nothing at all improper, cupping with one hand half the offering that had nothing at all to do with cookies and milk? Beyond doubt it was one of her big Irish bosoms inside the dress, and he considered changing his mind, throwing off the bolsters, rising in the stifling encouraging heat of the pink lamp and crossing the whitening and ever-widening fields and taking his place beside her on the bed with the long-legged doll. But no, he was mistaken, his was the strength to uphold logic and honor enough for the two of them if the big girl had succumbed to Toots's game and wanted to play. But then it came to him, *Irish body*, and he returned her wet smile, prepared to stand up, pajamas or no pajamas.

A rush of girlish naked feet—two pairs—the desperate fumbling sound of Toots's cold hands struggling with the knob, Toots and Virgie hurtling like slick-skinned harpies into the world of love. They knocked over the bowls, sent flying the green-eyed grapes, stilled the spouting waters of fat stone cherubs glistening around the pool.

Twenty minutes, he thought. Twenty minutes? Surely Toots had broken the rules of her own game, as he might have known she would.

"Well," said Toots, breathless, painfully squeezing Virgie's hand. "What happened?"

"Nothing," said Molly, without any trace of unkindness. "Next time will be different."

"You'll play again?" asked Toots.

"Yes," said Molly. "Once more. You'll enjoy yourself."

"Well," said Toots, tossing her head and walking out of the room, leaving wide the door and behind her the remains of cups and saucers and broken cakes. "I hope you're right."

And there was a next time. Only the following day. It was all the same except that Molly locked herself and Michael inside the little mock boudoir and unbuttoned her skirt from hem to above the knee before she sat down. She patted the bed beside her, he was able to stand, to cross the room, to perch himself so close to her that they touched. The warmth of her thigh warmed him, the breath that he found himself breathing cleared his lungs. She waited, she tipped him down onto the bed, one of his upflung hands encountering the long legs of the doll, and leaned over, put her lips to his. She had a handkerchief, an ordinary handkerchief that she had scented with the scent he had smelled the day before, and this she carefully worked into the fly of his pajama pants that would never button and that gave handkerchief and warm hand alike good access. She stuffed him as the doll was stuffed. Before he could reach for her and in the darkness behind his eyelids her fingers moved, the handkerchief moved, and in the sudden convulsion he did not care what her careful fingers did or how the handkerchief smothered him in touch and scent.

By the time Toots dragged Virgie up and down the staircases and around to the other door and entered the room in which nothing had changed, Molly had rebuttoned her skirt and pocketed her handkerchief crumpled around his little gift, as she later called it, while he was stroking the fat bolsters and regaining his breath.

When Toots demanded as before to know what had happened, Molly replied that she must wait to find out and that she would never find out if she did not help with the tea things.

* * *

Molly undertook still greater risks. Long after Aunt Alexandra had come to stroke his back as he lay propped on his pillows and wheezing, when he was half asleep and remembering both what the girl had done with him and how it had felt, while recalling what Aunt Alexandra always looked like late in the night—her red hair down upon the shoulders of a purple cashmere robe—his door opened. Someone entered, closed the door, for a moment stood quietly in the darkness, listening perhaps, as he was listening, to the sounds of the horses gently kicking the walls of their box stalls. The hounds were still. The small cathedral of his chest was quiet. Then the intruder took off her robe and naked, as he soon found out, entered his bed.

For a long while the darkness was lit with the bright flashes of fear and disbelief, though it was only he who had gone rigid and not the unimaginable intruder, since he could hear her slow and ordinary breathing and, despite the bedcovers, smell her as she must smell in the middle of any ordinary night. Then she rolled in his direction, nothing more, and the convulsion came. No hand, no fingers, no handkerchief. No time for him to move or think, nothing but the second convulsion, which, he knew later, was twice as consuming as the first.

He dozed, awoke and dozed, awoke and found his pajama jacket open and the pants untied. Up he started, wide-eyed, blinded again, but gently a heavy hand pushed against his chest until he let himself fall back to his pillows. How could she so imitate the mare, the lioness, the sleepy four-footed creature cleansing colt or cub? But suddenly, without warning, he heard himself trying to suppress a groan at the same time that he heard how odd it was to groan in a high register. It came to him that this time the missing handkerchief would make no difference. Still later, when he saw the grayish underside of the faintest light of the wet dawn and felt her moving, he perceived that there had been still another change—he the sailor, she the ship. And when he next awoke, she was gone.

The following night, sometime after she had arrived, listened, and entered his bed, manhood was his.

Grandfather's funeral filled the Van Fleet private cemetery. Black umbrellas formed an unruly shelter, a rough and rolling sea above the old tilting stones. Mourners packed themselves into the cold, wet cemetery, dismal with years and rain, as much for Grandfather's notoriousness as for his renown. The dirt road was barely passable for the family, only with the greatest self-denial did the mourners stand back and leave a misty space around this mausoleum that had been opened up for Grandfather.

All heads were bowed, all eyes peered out from beneath dripping umbrellas, dripping brims.

But the funeral was memorable not just for the size of its attendance but because of a special gift of flowers, an arrangement of fresh flowers that in the rain was as bright as Monet's palette. It stood as tall as a person beside the open door of the tomb, which contained just space enough for Grandfather's casket.

The crowd of mourners, the bell that was tolling for Grandfather, the expression on Uncle Harold's face as he helped to carry the casket—nothing quite caught the breath as did that gift of flowers. And why? It was in the shape of a horseshoe! A horseshoe of many-colored flowers for Grandfather!

4

"MIKE?" SHE SAID.

"Alex?"

"I need you," she said.

It was the darkest part of the night in my studio, three weeks after Hal's funeral. Four o'clock in the morning, as I discovered after the call. The windows were sealed, my fingers were reluctant on the switch, it was impossible to see in this total darkness. But the space beside me was soft and warm. Someone else had been lying in my bed that night. Who was she? Who had left me only moments before Alexandra's call?

"It's nothing emotional," said the familiar voice in my ear. "But I need you for two things. Or one, really."

"Alexandra," I said, "what can I do?"

"It's Harold," she said, so that for a moment I thought he was still alive. "I'm going to have a memorial hunt. It came to me just now. But the important thing is that I've had them install a photographer's studio. For you. An enormous place in the basement. Fully equipped. And I want you to do his biography—in photographs. Do you remember?"

"I don't seem to," I said. "But that's all right."

"He always wanted you to re-create his life in photographs," she said, and paused. Suddenly I knew she might be in her bed at Steepleton or might not. After all, night did not define Alexandra or confine her. She could just as well be dressed in jeans and sweater and calling me from her stable manager's office with Harry Martin sitting across from her and watching, listening. Or from the salon with her eyes on Whistlejacket, dimly lit. Or merely from her own safe bed, where she lay listening to the night and preferring not to sleep.

"I didn't know about the re-creation of Hal's life in photographs," I said, still propped on my arm and still preferring darkness to the light of the small black lamp on the floor.

"Oh, yes, he spoke of it often," she said in a voice that was not pleasing. And then, "The memorial hunt ought to last three days. The last three days of the month."

"You want me to combine the two," I said. "Prepare his pictorial biography, help you to honor him in the hunt. Grandly. In the right spirit."

"Yes," she said after another pause. "Yes, you understand. I need you, Virgie and I both need you. We just want you to live up here until we've all done our best for Hal."

She waited, I listened. But no telltale sound gave away the scene. It was mine to invent. I put her in her own bed where she belonged. Alone. Like me.

"Tomorrow," I said into the mouthpiece of my sculpted telephone, a crescent of shiny blackness I could feel but not see, "tomorrow. In the afternoon."

"Thanks," she said.

In the darkness, on the futon large enough for two, I waited, then allowed myself just enough light to note the hour. The sound of another clock would tell me when to get up, fold the futon, walk in my bare feet and Japanese-style gray pajamas to hot shower, hot shave, preparations for my drive to Steepleton. Recently my doctor had told me my feet were flat, despite my youth and the pride I took in my slenderness, and even the thought of bare feet brought a flush to my cheeks. Perhaps I should change doctors.

I had little to take except additional cameras because for the last ten years or since the summer I turned eighteen, I too have had a private apartment at Steepleton. It was then that Alexandra converted her father-in-law's rooms to my tastes and interests to surprise me, and thus that for a pleasing decade duplicate clothes, duplicate shoes and shaving things, duplicate shirts and riding boots, etc. have always awaited me in the rooms that once belonged to Walter T. Van Fleet.

In the darkness I reached for the warmth that had lingered beside me. It was gone. Before sleep came—I have never been afflicted with insomnia—I thought about Alexandra summoning me to Steepleton. It was because of me, I thought, that Hal had hit upon the unusual kind of immortality he would gain among us. Yes, he must have spoken of the plan when I was young, must have spoken of it to me as well as to Alexandra. There would be albums, I understood, containing my photographs and Harold's life.

Or part of it.

And the hunt?

A fitting tribute from a wife. Or was it?

Early in a springtime long ago Ashley arrived one morning in my studio. Early for her and early for many, but the rest of us were ready and waiting a good hour before she came up the second long flight of metal stairs toward my studio-loft, which smelled of coffee in paper cups and here and there reflected the morning light.

"Good morning, Ashley," I said as she pushed her way through the fire door, which with its weight and springs and panel of wired frosted glass was the fitting doorway after the dismal stairs and before the contemporary emptiness of my studio. The effort of her breathing showed, she had come to us directly from her bed. Or someone else's. No shower. No effort to take the sleep out of her face.

"You've got a reputation," she said as she accepted the cup, "I can see why." She leaned against a long white wall, looked at me, at my black pants and white T-shirt and bare feet. She glanced about once for signs of personal effects—she knew I lived in my studio—then back to me. Perhaps she thought I was dressed for the beach. "But I want to tell you," she said after a pause, "I'm going to lunch. Important. So you won't take long. Will you?" She dropped the cup in a heavy metal wastebasket.

"Not long," I said.

She was tall, she wore tight jeans, this early in the morning she was, I thought, both tough and gawky. Inappropriate for spring colors. But I trusted Alice.

I had talked with the others before Ashley arrived. I decided I wanted only a muddy green for background, the color that a cow's hoof sinks into in the first warm golden light of the sun, and we had hung our pea-green, field-green paper over one of the narrower walls. White umbrellas would flood Ashley in a diffusion of soft light, my portrait of her would start from the center and hold the eye.

Makeup. Clothes. Rhoda, my assistant, and Jane and Edith. A crescent of equipment, no natural light, the long table, a chair, Jane's white coat. A Japanese screen.

I could see Ashley's head and elbows over the top of the screen. Exactly when she had removed her old sweater and man's white shirt and had hung shirt and sweater over the edge of the screen, I interrupted. I told her to take a shower. She objected. I insisted. She followed me, clutching the shirt to her chest, and was surprised when I showed her the tiled walls and floors, the glass doors, the dressing table, the bulbs around the mirror. When I pointed to the towels, I told her the idea was not cleanliness but mood, washing it all away except herself, the young woman whose face couldn't be absolutely right unless it acquired the light of a shower freshly taken.

She came back swinging her shirt and pleased with herself. The jeans were tight to traces of steam on her lower body, she had taken the trouble to refasten her blue silk bra. She looked less than ever like the model I should have had for the colors of spring, for the girl or woman who attracts other girls and women to pink. But she sat down at the table, Jane dried her hair, not thoroughly, and I began to see the first shadings of innocence in her Nebraskan face.

Jane leaned over Ashley, brushed and painted so that the dry, white, slightly puffy face of an uncooperative model became softly fluid in sandy beige, acquired lines of thinnest plum around the eyes. And the lips—Jane colored Ashley's lips with a lipstick that was a crush, a sheen of golden apples and slippery peach.

Ashley made a sarcastic comment about pink. Edith, complaining about the time, helped Ashley try on this pink blouse or that one.

"Take off the bra," I said. "How am I going to do anything with that blue bra clashing with the pink?"

"What?" she said, surprised then scornful again. "But you can't see it!"

"But I can see it," I said softly. "Don't you understand? You can go behind the screen if you have to."

Edith guided her behind the Japanese screen, she emerged with pink cuffs folded, breasts visible beneath the pink fabric that belonged to the pleated skirt of a girl in the spring. But she was angry.

As with certain horses of bad posture or dull temper, she was deliberately making herself slack—arms, legs, shoulders, facial expression—in front of the yellow and greenish muck of the background and in the light reflected from the white umbrellas.

"What about the hat?" Edith asked suddenly in all the inspiring accents of her native tongue, which was French, and I turned to it, a frivolous pseudocanvas hat for girls on bicycles or girls carrying books by leather straps. "Do you think this dreadful hat might help?" It was orange. If I had complained of blue and pink, how much more violent the clash between pink and orange?

For answer I simply took the hat and leveled it on Ashley's head.

"This is the worst sitting I've ever had," she said.

"Edith," I said, "what's wrong with it?"

"Turn up the brim," she said. "In front."

I did so, Rhoda was ready to switch on the lights but I stopped her, stepped away from the camera. Then, carefully, I eased Rhoda's French eyeglasses off her face and onto Ashley's. Rhoda always wore scholastic-looking eyeglasses, but this morning I noticed them only thanks to the hat. Then the lights as pure and white as the face of a glacier held Ashley's face in place. The lights went dark, Edith draped a rosy heavy-knit sweater over Ashley's shoulders, tied the sleeves just under the throat. Ashley was wearing two pink flannelette shirts, but I could still see her breasts beneath them. The square-shaped eyeglasses were the color of petrified wood highly polished.

I spoke as kindly as I could to Ashley then, camera clicking. I told her that she was becoming monochromatic. Pink to orange, golden sand to peach in a bottle of liqueur. I said that everything I saw was in a sense the same. Even the shadows. I told Ashley that her face was framed in dark green shadows that picked up the background and her eyebrows and eyes. I said that her eyes were interesting, and so they were—different, nearly black. But, I said, as close as I was to the face in my lens, I could see no center, no starting place. What, I asked, was the viewer of the printed photograph to look at? Clothes and cosmetics like a Navajo sunrise, a nice artificiality of colors. But the face didn't match the shirts and sweater, the silly hat. Didn't bring to the portrait any pertness, sex.

"It's too bad this photograph doesn't allow for the inclusion of your bottom half," I said, and she came to life.

"Wait—" she started to say, and there it was, the look of the *w* on Ashley's lips, the first of many.

"Don't speak," I said, as close to her as I could get, "but keep doing it. *Weather, wilderness, warm, what, whoa.* It's like pursing your mouth for a kiss. But that's not what you're doing," I said. "Shall I tell you—"

"Don't," she said, interrupting us both, surprising herself as well as me, I think, "don't tell me."

"You felt it," I said. "No pretenses, Ashley. But we're finished, we have our center. Not a viewer's eye but will start with the round of darkness between your puckered lips."

What followed was brief and in slow motion. She removed the frivolous hat and dropped it, I removed the eyeglasses and handed them back to Rhoda. Ashley moistened her lips. Jane recovered the missing wristwatch near one of my electric razors, Ashley merely thrust it into a tight pocket. Then with a single hurt glance at me she was gone. Edith had left us long before.

* * *

The photograph that was finally selected of Ashley in pink pleased everyone, offended none. It was skillfully silly. Who could complain of Ashley's mouth and bright fish-lips? But Ashley and I both knew that the surprise she mimed in our first photograph was senseless. More than senseless. For days and weeks after taking that photograph I detested pink. Pink in every shade and form. Sliced strawberries. Red-rimmed eyes. Rare meat. All the innocent, provocative tones I saw in mirrors or in small outdoor gardens beginning to flourish beneath high walls. And yet around this time I became obsessed with faces. Faces were my excuse to lavish hidden skills and personal interests on the mouths and lips of models justifiably, without resorting to fantasies no one else could see.

There was the tawny-haired lioness from whose wide, full, plum-colored lips I coaxed the sliest smile. And the older woman whose flat white face I framed in the broad leaves of pink orchids in order to concentrate on the sadness in her expressionless bright orange lips. Foreign models or models whose appearance reflected foreign cultures swept me through the next four photographs. A gorgeous, proud, pouting girl whose head and face I decked out masterfully in a wig of tight black curls and an obviously old straw hat with a black band. The chin is resting on a hand in a loosely crocheted white glove in turn propped on the silver head of a slender black walking stick. The photograph is for the most part black and gray. And despite the white of the glove, the soft corn color of the straw hat, the almost fierce black look of the eyes, the deadly elegance of this young woman, it is the mouth that once again remains the center. Broad. Highlighted with slivers of light and on one side of the upper lip shadows that might be soft hair. Now it is the suggestion of the sensual pout that is the art.

All this good fortune included two French models and photographs that were not confined to heads and faces. First there is the two-page study in blue and black of the girl propped on her forearm on a quay in a slight rain. The model's knees are partially raised, she wears black stockings and dark blue shoes—one foot lies half on its side, my inspiration of that day—and we see several bowlike shapes of net thrust up where the skirt is raised, an edge of provocative bare midriff. But this pose is best because the girl's black hair sweeps into the rest of her prone darkness, though the hair is bunchy and hardly shoulder-length, while the face is upturned. She lies on gray slats—she complained of those wet slats—there is water beyond her and beyond the water, which is also out of focus, a hint of green shore and indecent villas. Shouldn't the girl's languid proneness on a slippery quay be sufficient to provoke us? Are not her body and the splash of black artificiality of clothing enough to satisfy our desire? But no, it is not her inviting pose but rather her small, white, upturned face with—absolutely—its thick-lipped mouth dominating every detail I included in the photograph down to the zipper that opens her two-toned jacket that someone has cleverly turned inside out. No matter how large the photograph, how much of stockinged calf and thigh and windblown hair we see, still it is the mouth that makes our heads swing, our interest rise.

The second French photograph of that period—when I was what? aged twenty or so?—I must take more seriously. It was also to be printed as a two-page spread and was, I had been told, to be provocative.

This work was done in a restaurant, in midmorning and well before lunch had been served and while the restaurant was still empty. The girl was big-boned, sultry, unfriendly, and French in name and appearance only, nothing more. Her dark hair was heavy for her narrow face and exposed her neck and shoulders. Despite her size and height, she had a slender neck, nearly serpentine, and a shy face and straight or actually sharp nose. And the big, sensual mouth. I could see nothing except her lips, but it was obvious that here was a woman who combined deerlike fragility with broad shoulders and a handsome knee. Her broad and powerful knee was ripe for the hand or would be as quickly as I could expose it, which would not be long.

We used two large tables. The nearest I arranged so that it suggested four luncheons already eaten and brought to mind three departed guests—simply by filling four large wineglasses to different levels with red wine. That's all it took. The second table I left in the background with its places set, its wineglasses upside down and waiting. Both tables were draped in white linen tablecloths, the chairs were black wood.

Now for the model. I told her to sit at the nearest table and to my left, or to the left of the camera, and she needed no encouragement, no instructions to sit with one arm hooked over the back of the chair and her left arm flat on the table so that the fingers of her left hand touch the stem of her glass half filled with ruby red. She sprawls. She is a natural sprawler. Indolent. Her fingers are about to twirl the glass.

She is wearing an ivory-colored cashmere set—a collarless top tight to the body and over that a sweater, also collarless with buttonholes like perfectly spaced small surgical slits and glass buttons, the sweater worn open and edged with silver—all this with a black sarong. It was the slit in the sarong that enabled me to show a full portion of knee and calf, which caught the deepest orange and gold tones of my filters and hence held the entire photograph at its lower edge. I filled our corner of the restaurant with a deep golden-orange color appropriate to the desert across which her captors had carried her.

I leaned forward and flicked her hair lightly until her left eye was hidden and the right eye couldn't help but be menacing. She wore five heavy diamond bracelets on each wrist. I cast a long, sharp shadow down the right side of her nose, and this shadow meets the largest curl of black hair, the one that hides the eye.

And yet the treasure of that photograph was Sylvia's mouth—yes, it was she—the slightly parted lips so unusually fat and full as to be not merely the sign of a seductive nature but, as I discovered when we left the restaurant, her constant source of embarrassment. To think that Sylvia was and is embarrassed by her protuberant lips!

The pasty red of her lips, the glasses of wine, the thickness of the orange knee—these are the elements that hold the eye in the Algerian light.

It is one of my best photographs. I am proud of it. I

finished it quickly so that Sylvia and I could drink the wine and leave together as the scent of the chef's preparations reached us still more strongly on a hot wind.

My array of mouths, my study of lips end intentionally with the mouth and lips of a horse.

Of course, the girl on his back should have been my subject. But the girl's face was nondescript, she was not a serious rider, the horse was a fine gray animal that should not have been made to carry such a girl.

We were outdoors, I squatted, I took the photograph so that the horse towered above me like some spotted gray sinuous sea monster. The girl is wearing a white shirt, brown riding britches. Her brown hair is long and blows out horizontally between her own head and the horse's. She carries a fly switch, I caught her with a brief triangle of light between her crotch and the invisible saddle. But the art of it was this: I startled the horse. Startled him. With a snap of the fingers. Up he went, the girl yanked back on the reins, she twisted his silvery head to the side, a purplish eye as large as a plum stared down at me in hatred, or possibly fear, while the girl looked off to the side. At least she managed not to fall.

But there's the horse, his open mouth. The lips are wide, thick, rubbery, pulled only partly open by the painful bit and the yank of the reins. In the width of the horse's mouth is a line of foam, two teeth revealed by the open lips look like pieces of carrot.

The girl was no match for the horse, though vanity kept her in the saddle. Vanity and luck. The horse was not a Thoroughbred. But the photograph showed promise.

Lunch at The Flying Crane, dinner at The Red Chamber. Japanese, Chinese. Occasionally The Pearl, The Shanghai Inn. Nothing but Asian food for Carol and me.

Tonight The Red Chamber. Black and white decor with mirrors. The floors, whether raised a step or flat from start to finish, consist of large black and white squares while about half the doors are surfaced with mirrors. The ceiling and three out of four walls are solid black so that the entire place, including bar and tabletops, is a brightly polished discontinuous uniformity dimly lit by small chrome-plated lamps whose light is a pale pink.

Ten o'clock of a spring evening. I was dressed in an ordinary gray suit appropriate to the season and to any young man in business since I prefer neither to look nor to act like a photographer. But not Carol. Tight black patent leather slippers, off-white slacks, a red T-shirt, and a jacket of smudged and faintly shiny black that hung not quite to her knees. Carol is a professional model who has always looked like one.

Crowded. At the polished black bar and facing a mirror. Carol was sitting to my right, a man—someone we didn't know—was sitting to Carol's right. To my left was a vase of delphiniums, an incongruous mass of blue and white flowers on long stalks rising from a collar of ferns around the top of the vase. And for the final touch a select few purple irises and white daisies that touched off the blue and white with dabs of yellow and orange that belonged in a field. In the mirror across the space at times invaded by a man or boy with trays, my favorite flowers in their tall yet chunky vase looked as if they had just been done in oils fresh from the palette. An old Impressionist and his erotic flowers.

To my left was the last seat in our row. An undesirable claustrophobic seat that abutted the wall. Anyone squeezed into that last seat could see straight ahead into the mirror, could see the intrusion of the flowers. But could see nothing of the face of the unacknowledged acquaintance seated to the immediate right. Whereas I, the silent neighbor, had a full view of the other's face in the mirror, thanks to my increased distance from the black wall and hence enlarged angle of sight. The vase of flowers stood between us. The advantage was mine. I was able to look straight into the mirror and yet with a quick and comfortable shift of my eyes to the left—all undetected—survey my unmade acquaintances as they came and went. And talk constantly to Carol.

Sudden vacancy. One moment an uninteresting older woman, the next moment nothing. Fading scent, empty stool. I looked away.

Carol said something, I answered, the man on Carol's right started speaking to her.

Then, at last, a newcomer. A woman, as I knew before looking at her in the mirror. I felt her squeezing in, settling herself. The boy whose tray was always empty was off to the far right and hardly visible. Carol laughed, answered the man. I hadn't heard what they were saying, but I laughed as well. Then I gave a glance to my left.

She was young but no girl. Her expression said that if she could have seen my face, she would have apologized for squeezing against me. She was that kind of woman. Honest, uncertain, ordinary. But she must have known where she was dining that night because she was wearing a linen suit of black and white check and a tight blue jersey with a round neck. She was not a model, her features were not distinctive, nonetheless she had intelligence enough to duplicate in her clothing the decor of The Red Chamber.

"It's a crowded night," I said.

She smiled into the mirror, looked down.

"Have you ever thought that each of us is a menu?" I asked.

"Why, no," she answered, trying to see me through the flowers.

"I should have said Chinese menu," I said.

"It makes a difference," she said.

Her face was soft, large, neither square nor round, her lips were not full enough to hold my attention. Her voice might have belonged to any number of women.

"The person as menu," I said, "is not a hierarchical arrangement. We wouldn't concentrate on eyes before lips, lips before tongue, throat before hands."

"I don't think I understand," she said.

"Parts of the body," I said. "Menu. The Western menu is prearranged so that we are not free to begin where we wish or to value equally what we're eating. It's fixed. In the West we eat by formula, proceeding swiftly through any number of unappreciated, even hardly tasted concoctions in order to reach the climactic dish, then are eased down from it none too gently, all the way to the finger bowl."

She nodded. I was watching her in the mirror.

"And," I said, "to our Western minds a finger bowl is something most people don't even bother to rinse their fingers in. And, of course, there's the Western taboo that forbids drinking from the finger bowl."

She laughed.

To my right was an immediate vacancy. No Carol. A vacancy and then the man. Well-manicured fingers, a swizzle stick. Carol gone to the phone or *Women*.

"But some of us," I said, "want only to break that taboo. Water, lemon, chilled silver."

Again she laughed.

"So the Western menu limits how we please our appetites. Imprisons the whole thing, makes it monotonous, dull, uninspired, uninteresting, banal, unarousing. Whereas the Eastern menu gives us free choice. Choice means variable, variable means discontinuity, discontinuity destroys hierarchy."

"It doesn't sound very passionate to me," she said.

I was surprised.

"Logic is the way to erotic truth," I said.

"All right," she said. "But tell me more about the menu."

"Kamaboko," I said. "Shabu Shabu. Igaguri."

"Those are Japanese dishes!" she cried. "We're in a Chinese restaurant. Remember?"

"I remember," I said.

"What you mean," she said slowly, "is that in our case it doesn't matter."

I did not answer. Behind her, in the mirror, there was now the torso of a heavily built man. Jacket, white shirt, flower in the buttonhole. No head. She saw him also and began to push back her stool. Carol, I realized, was twirling her glass.

Silence. Noise.

"You must have enjoyed talking with her."

"But you were in *Women*. Or phoning."

"Oh, I've been back awhile."

"You were doing a lot of talking yourself."

"He left."

"Ready to eat?"

Alex and the portrait of Whistlejacket await me in the salon. She sits on one Chippendale chair, props her muddied boots on another, and stares at the horse. And I am hurrying. I drive in the outside lane. I see exactly what's before me, around me, and am not distracted by what I see of the past, brief glimpses of the models—five in number, I count them—who struck their poses early in my professional career and still do. Susan. Carol. Ashley. Sylvia. Bonnie. What's become of Susan and Bonnie? Gone, both of them, though I first photographed Bonnie on a Caribbean island and Susan encouraged me to call her Sooz. But they'll return. So it's Carol? Carol. Or the two Carols I met at the same time. Or almost.

A pain in my tooth. A molar. An insufferable pain in that beautiful white molar that had never known a crack or cavity. So I argued with my dentist as never before when he recommended I see an endodontist to discuss, which meant undergo as it turned out, my first root canal. I insisted that I was too young to have a root canal. He said not at all. I said the tooth was as healthy as a lamb. He said I'd lose it at one one-thousandth of a second if I didn't get over to the endodontist.

Early one morning I met him along with his assistant—a brief and guarded introduction—and the receptionist, who was young but new on the job and looked it. The endodontist—it was the word that lured me to him, nothing else— had spoken with my dentist and wanted to talk about photographing miracles. He had a way of turning his body halfway through a sentence so that a full view of him gave way to his right side, the back of his head, full face, by the time he had started on another sentence. His disclaimers about pain were richer and loftier than I'd ever heard. But deliberately not credible. He meant the patient to see through his exaggerations. And soon I realized that the reason he kept shifting his face—by turning his white-coated body as though it were an upright spindle—was that the right side of it had been crushed. Next I saw that his head and face appeared to be composed of nodes and nodules and that these physical disfigurations accounted for his sardonic disposition.

There came the third and fourth sessions with no end in sight—after he had promised quick work of my perfect

white molar, which, he had made me believe, contained a
flaming cancerous pulp inside its deceptive enamel, though
the second adjective was metaphorical, as he assured me. I
lessened my guard about the pain, concentrated both on his
curious little instruments and on his assistant, Carol. She
wore bobbed hair and white pants and tunic, talked in a
voice that was not a whisper but was nonetheless too low in
volume for me to understand but just right, I gathered, for
the endodontist. She was thin, shy, she spoke softly, without
inflection. It was precisely her lack of feminine qualities that
aroused my interest, along with the endodontist's possessive manner despite Carol's unmistakable gold ring. Could
she possibly be married to him? A shake of the head. But
she was married. A quiet yes.

At the end of the fourth session he joked with me—while
drawing sick fluid from my boyish molar—about how some-
day Carol was going to leave him. She was behind my
back—another of his sinister habits was to keep her well out
of the patient's sight. Nonetheless he made his joke and from
behind me came the answer. I looked straight up into his flat
intolerable light and heard her.

"Would it matter?"

No inflection. Spoken as softly and clearly as his light
above my face was fierce. Why was I so moved by what
could only be heard as the most obvious of innuendos? And
expressed in a way that allowed for the possibility that Carol
meant what she said? That endodontist had made me wait
three long sessions and most of a fourth stretched out
beneath his bad breath and sinister manner before using me
in order to make an innuendo about his assistant, who could
not have weighed 108 pounds. But it was her answer—her
cool, soft-spoken answer that I could hear for once—that
made me twist my head, despite the sudden unbreakable
grip of his fingers on my jaw and face, and attempt to see
her, which I could not. I listened; he leaned over me; I paid
no attention to his deplorable breath.

Weeks later there came our fifth rendezvous, which I now
anticipated with guard completely down and my interest in
Carol firmly fixed. I was twenty-one or -two years old, she
was about the same. Once, when leaving after an earlier

appointment in that office, I prolonged the moment of saying good-bye to the receptionist, who had learned nothing about me despite my repeated visits. Carol returned, as I knew she would, and gave the receptionist some obviously invented message. I said my good-byes to Carol instead of to the receptionist but rather than voice a reply, she merely raised one stiff hand and forearm in a crisp salute, then strode back to the endodontist.

Saluted by Carol! At the beginning of the fifth session I had her salute, her bobbed hair, her thin body concealed in white, and, most of all, her voice well in mind. Her job, aside from talking with the endodontist, was mainly to arrange his little hand-held drills and to pass them along when he requested them, which was often in the surliest of tones. A red plastic-handled drill—the handle only large enough to hold between thumb and forefinger—looked like a small portion of a serrated needle, but once inside the growing cave of my molar it felt like a three-pound iron rasp. He twisted his fingers, the little drill twirled, the reverberations sounded throughout my head.

"You know," he said, addressing me directly, which he rarely did, "I've been thinking how easily I could commit a murder. You, for instance. Do you realize that you're absolutely in my power? And how easily I could do you in, as they say?"

He was joking, or trying to, perched on the stool at my side and every now and then interrupting himself to murmur something, in his humorless professional voice, to Carol. His white tunic was like a fencer's and he wore it open at the throat, cavalierly. His face was damaged, his hair was black, he was average in his height, his build. His ears stuck out. The black hair on his forearms protruded thickly from beneath the white and slightly unclean cuffs. An unsavory man. Sadistic. Devious. Like his profession.

"For all you know," he said, sitting upright a moment, legs spread, giving himself a little rest, "you might be my victim already. The kind of murder I'm talking about takes time. Suppose that whenever I've washed out one of your root canals—remember that this tooth has three of them—the solution has been of chlorine as usual plus arsenic. That's how simple it is. I clean out the roots as I go, the arsenic is absorbed into the bloodstream, in a few months you die. No one suspects poisoning—why should they?—and no one is going to suspect your endodontist. He's beyond reproach, he has no motive. How's that?"

My mouth was full of his fingers, he hadn't given me enough local anesthetic.

"Do you talk this way to all your patients?" I managed to say.

"As a matter of fact I don't," he said. "Just you."

"Why," I mumbled, feeling his imaginary arsenic beginning to work, "why me?"

"Oh, I don't know," he said. "You just strike me as the type. I don't mean you're a likely person to hear my plan. I mean you're the kind of young man who might be a likely first. First victim." Then reaching across and behind me, "Shall we kill him, Carol?"

"Count me out," came the faint, clear voice, and the endodontist flushed, smiled one of his false smiles, gripped my jaw, and, holding the oversize plastic syringe so that I could see it, prepared to give me another rinse of chlorine.

I thought of Carol sitting near me though out of sight, my witness to this fellow's sadistic tendencies, and I smelled his bad breath, twisted to get a better glimpse of him, tried to determine what had smashed his face. A former patient? An automobile accident? A rival for his wife's affections? The thirty or forty little drills with their bright handles, tips down and all lined up like cribbage pieces, were enough to warp his personality.

And then the bony, hairy wrist cut my line of vision, he scowled, with a strong thumb he drove in the plunger.

"Wait!" I cried. "Stop!"

Burning! Fire on ice! Sensation of scalding! And in a single rivulet the pain shot from tooth to nose, to eyes, to roof of the mouth, to back of the throat, burning away like hot wires, like fire that cannot be quenched. I gagged, I struggled to sit upright. He held me down. I broke away.

"Do something!" I cried. "I'm burning!"

"Where's your courage?" he asked, sitting upright again

and resting his palms on his thighs. "You've been through this before. It's just chlorine."

"Chlorine? Chlorine!" I cried. "You pushed too hard! You forced that chlorine right through the tip of the root! It's filling my head and dripping down the back of my throat. Like acid!"

"Well," he said, "it happens. It stings because it's in the sinus ducts. It's uncomfortable but nothing to worry about."

"You better worry," I said. "You've destroyed my olfactory nerves and God knows what else. That's plenty to worry about."

"Well," he said, "the only problem is the delay. We'll have to wait a couple of weeks so it'll heal. Carol," he added in a cheerful voice, "let him rinse."

He left us. For some reason he shut the door. And in one long motion slender, lithe Carol came from behind me, raised the chair, lifted the armrest, tilted the overhead light out of the way, nudged the vacated stool aside, leaned down, and held the paper cup to my lips. My nostrils burned, my eyes were watering. What could be more vulnerable than the tissues of the nasal and oral cavities? On the wall across from me the photograph of the yacht under full sail and spanking the seas, her skipper—a young woman in a captain's cap— stood spread-legged behind the wheel. She was dressed like Carol except for the addition of the blue cap. The Skipper. The crisp salute.

"Rinse," she said. "Expectorate. They teach us that 'expectorate' is a better word than 'spit.' I don't agree."

"Say it then," I mumbled in the midst of my burning. "Spit."

"Spit," she said, and as easily as an uncoiling wave or pennant slid onto my lap. Glass, steel, the needles that were the teeth of this trade, jars of cotton, drill bits for the supersonic drills—there were two—and in beautiful contrast here was Carol, suddenly, on my lap. She was as light as a white leaf, her white clinging trousers were of a stretch fabric like the richest silk.

"Carol," I said, but she was up and away without a wrinkle, without a trace of emotion, not a tease, I realized, but practical. For an instant I saw the shape of her underpants embossed on the seat of her trousers, still felt in the tips of my fingers the cool bareness of her narrow waist. She washed her hands—another instant of her unsmiling humor—rattled a few instruments. I was hardly aware of the swimming pool taste in my mouth and nose.

"Still here?" the endodontist suddenly asked from the doorway. "I need you, Carol. Didn't you hear the buzz?"

"Coming," she said in a voice I could not hear, but he was gone.

I wrote my address on his prescription pad, she put her hand on my arm. Then I too was gone.

I never took Carol's photograph. Rather I did not take photographs of Carol the endodontist's assistant. Carol the model has been my subject since I was first betrayed by a molar. The model looks nothing like the girl in white, whom I have not seen in years. However, the first Carol and I discussed more than once the photographs I might have taken of her. Carol dressed only in high heels and a copper-colored half slip and posed in the endodontist's chair. Carol with her tunic open and one hand raised to her dark bobbed hair. Carol in her tight white pants and bending over. Carol brushing her shiny hair in the endodontist's mirror, her cosmetics stacked on the bone-white china surface of one of the instrument trays. Carol's thin thighs astraddle the narrow chair. "Doctor" and Carol in a half-nude embrace with the movable overhead light still burning but knocked into a hasty useless angle. We laughed over our photographs in which she and I would occasionally pose together or in which she would wear only the tunic of her official uniform and, at a jaunty angle, the seagoing cap.

One late afternoon Carol appeared in my studio-loft, camera in hand. It was she who would take the pictures, she said, and she demanded to pose me as she wished. A Polaroid camera bought for the occasion. An amateur's surprising skill. Her pictures did me justice, and whenever she allowed me to share a brief glance at them, we did not laugh. Carol's pictures marked the progress of our friendship, which ended, as I knew it must, the day I requested that she give me a sampling of her pictorial record and she refused. At least Carol gave me an early lesson: the reserve of a lean figure promises a woman of sudden passion and inventive mind. Of course I was secretly pleased that she wanted to keep my pictures to herself. Who wouldn't have been?

It is the photographer who counts and not his model. The mind of the photographer. Without time to think, without self-consciousness, without time for this choice or that, in time so brief it belongs only to photography itself, the person with the camera concentrates like no one else. He sees the picture before he takes it, he knows what it will look like before he sees the finished print. He sees what no ordinary person sees. Convention prohibits speaking intimately to strangers of the opposite sex and yet there are those, no matter how few, who are able to say anything they wish to strangers. Sudden intimate speech and behavior is a rare gift. And the photographer, or the kind of photographer I have in mind, intrudes into convention in the same way except with sight, not speech, though sometimes both.

It is my fortune or misfortune to see everyday sights as if holding the camera up to my eye even when I am not giving photography a thought. And no camera is made that accommodates both eyes in the viewfinder. Only one. In this case the sight of one eye is better than two. With one eye I am able to see light in total darkness. In the darkness my glass of wine is the deepest and brightest of ruby reds. But is such wine only to be drunk, not seen?

We'll see.

5

To A BOY'S eye Harold O. Van Fleet was the perfect figure of a father. He was tall but not heavy, his narrow wolfish face was always friendly, his favorite stance was with his feet apart and his back slightly swayed so as to give himself relief from the pain he always felt in his back. He had not injured himself in a fall from a horse, as might have been expected from such a man, but rather had risen too quickly one day while stooping under a whitewashed fence. The lines of his clothes were straight, with his tailored shirts he wore hand-knit ties, he had received his tiepin, a pale blue oval bearing in its center the head of a Russian wolfhound, early in his life from his own father, the famous Walter T. Van Fleet. Best of all, he wore a corset. His pink hunting coat, his several pairs of thin black boots with their brown tops, his hunting whips of braided thongs and bone handles—these were nothing compared with the corset, which, exactly like a woman's, was laced up the back.

One of Michael's earliest pleasures was lacing Uncle Harold's corset. It was a stiff bone-colored affair which, thanks to its white laces spaced closely up the back and supported at well-chosen spots by little straps and buckles, afforded Uncle Harold the pleasure and comfort he needed in light of the spasm, never far off, which, as he was fond of telling Michael, had shot through his spine like a bolt that day when he straightened up too soon and took the bottom edge of the plank across his back. He was paralyzed immediately—no fall from a horse had ever done him such desperate damage—and remained so for months. Gradually he learned to stand, he accepted the cane which told everyone who saw him that at best he had entered the world of the invalid and, at worst, that of premature old age. But he humbled himself, he learned to walk again, he helped himself along the corridors of Steepleton, steadying himself with the cane and on the arm of a young servant girl who had long preceded those who had cared for his father. He stooped, the pain was fierce, he dragged himself toward recovery. The corset was worse than the cane, and for days he refused to try it on. But Alexandra told him that the corset made his trim figure look even trimmer. He acquiesced. He began to enjoy his secret—that beneath the dashing clothes was the garment fit for a woman, that the tall, lithe build everyone admired was artificially achieved. The corset made him an even grander man than he was before the humiliating accident, which he tried to forget. Surely he deserved something better than the plank in that fence. Well might he have had a wet day, horses massed in the field, witnesses to describe later his courage in the face of the brutal fall he had taken. A hunting accident was understandable. Risk was inevitable on horseback. But he had only himself to blame for that white fence. Of course he could have suffered paralysis for life, which was not the case.

Michael would listen and gently pull at the laces, carefully following Uncle Hal's instructions and all the while marveling at the extent of the man, at his height, at the length and musculature of the back that needed corseting. The ribs were visible and allowed for deep breathing, the marks the corset had made in Uncle Hal's flesh the day before were still there despite the interval of the night. And the pain, as Michael knew, was never entirely gone, though Uncle Hal only complimented himself on the straight shoulders and manly bearing that he owed in part to the corset. It fitted

him like a glove, he said, and he would wear it until the day
he died.

Harold's first disappointment in life was Toots, his first
daughter. He had wanted and expected sons. He had done
his best to train his girls to his own passion, horses, but it
was a doomed effort. Toots had proven recalcitrant from the
outset and had never acquired the Van Fleet "seat," which
was painfully evident by the time of her sixteenth year. She
was stoop-shouldered no matter her extensive training in
dressage. Hal was perfectly aware that Toots had no apti-
tude for riding, but even worse, that she jeered at horses.
Furthermore, he watched in horror as his first daughter grew
into not only his own likeness but its parody. Where his own
shoulders reflected the pride of an upstanding man, his
daughter's sagging shoulders were a sign of personal indif-
ference. In Toots his own lean tallness became mere skinni-
ness, generally unpleasing and in a girl offensive. When he
looked at Toots, he saw his own narrow face grinning back at
him, shrunken to the bone in meanness. Once when Toots
had a particularly vicious argument with Alexandra, which
left the skinny girl white-faced and trembling, he had taken
the child walking up and down the driveway in front of
Steepleton with his arm around her shoulders and his peace-
maker's voice soft and consoling. But that was the extent of
any physical display of affection for Toots on Harold's part.

As for Virgie, she was a good little rider but otherwise too
weak and complaining to suit her father. Furthermore, her
undisguised love of Harold was more than any man could
bear. It was excessive, cloying. She ran to him, she clung to
his legs whenever she could, and he was repelled. Having
Virgie trying to hang on to your legs, he once confessed to
Alexandra, was worse than having a cat under your feet. His
voice softened when he saw Alexandra's distress, and he
apologized with honest fervor and promised to try to be a
good father somehow. But it was no use. He gave up
instructing Virgie on her pony, he avoided Toots. At least he
did his best to conceal his distaste for Alexandra's girls, as he
thought of them, but that was all.

Michael was as thin as the girls and less vulnerable. His smile was pure, his shyness was not offensive, he was tall, he was an agreeable boy whose greatest asset in the Van Fleet family was a startling affinity with the horse. He knew the number of teeth in the mouth of the adult horse—forty—and could name every bone and muscle in its body. He had read Xenophon on *The Art of Horsemanship*, he knew the theories about the migration of the horse and its development—from Europe to Mongolia and from little animals knee-high to the mammoth Percheron. In his dreams he saw running horses silhouetted against orange skies, saw their shoulders working, their hooves striking fire, heard them thundering in his direction, coming closer. In the presence of the living animals, in barn or field, he was cautious, trusting, delighted. He rode with daring, quickness of mind, consideration. Harold had only to see Michael walking into Steepleton to recognize him for what he was—horseman. A gifted horseman in the guise of a slight boy.

They hacked together across stubbled fields and down country lanes, sometimes accompanied by Alexandra, more often not. Michael worked his pony, Chuckers, under Harold's tutelage in the arena and outdoors in one of the rings. Harold watched with pride as Michael, hands on hips and without a saddle, took the unruly Chuckers over lively jumps. If the boy fell, Harold caught the pony and on they went. The fat Chuckers became trimmer, Michael as sure of his balance as a tightrope walker, spills, as Harold called them, or no spills.

There came the day of Michael's first hunt. The sky was bright, the temperature had fallen unseasonably, and even by late morning, when riders and horses were assembling in the courtyard of the Steepleton stables, the air against the skin was like ice on iron. The courtyard rang with great cheer; Will, who was mortally afraid of horses, passed among them, carrying trays of brandy shoulder-high, booted legs and mammoth rumps knocking against him. There was laughter, beneath the clear sound of the voices came the tinkling of curb chains, snorting, the muted ring of a freshly shod hoof on the cobblestones.

Michael was mounted on a large dark bay called Turf,

since Chuckers was lame, and he was elated that on this day he was not sitting with his head at the level of the trim hips or waists of the adults. Now he sat taller than most of the women smoking last cigarettes and drinking brandy. Turf was a former racehorse bought by Harold on his father's advice several years before the old man had died, and Harold and the young stable master, Harry Martin, had speculated long and thoughtfully as to whether or not Michael had the strength and experience to handle a horse of this kind. Turf was known for his roller-coaster gait, good disposition, and for having no faults except one. The bay, more black than brown and standing unusually tall at the withers—seventeen hands—had one fault only. His enthusiasm could overcome his training, his common sense, so that on the rarest occasion he could seize the bit in his teeth and run for it. Hal and Harry and Michael had stood beside the trustworthy horse and talked. Hal told Michael to be careful, Harry explained the problem, Hal said to hold this horse whatever he did, Harry said that once he took it into his head to go there was no stopping him. One miscalculation, said Harry, and a full-grown man couldn't hold him. Still, Turf was the best horse they had for Michael.

"Look at you," said Aunt Alexandra, bumping suddenly against him and reaching out, touching his arm with her gloved hand, smiling, "a handsome rider for such a handsome horse." She was wearing a black coat, as was most of the party, including himself, and canary britches and a length of white silk ribbon tied around the hatband of her high silken black hat. Its ends were fluttering down the back of her head almost to her velvet collar, what he could see of her auburn hair was as brushed and as tinged with gold as the coat of Hollyhock, her large chestnut mare.

He caught Uncle Harold's glance across the courtyard and the Master of Foxhounds in his red coat raised his whip-carrying hand to the peak of his black velvet hunting cap in a manly salute. Turf gave a tug on the reins.

They started off, rattling and jostling, their faces flushed and linen crisp, the black and tan hounds swarming ahead of them. Virgie on her Shetland pony and in the care of Buse was among them, well out of the crowd. The pair would skirt the hunt so that Virgie, at the edge of a field, could see her father and the rest of the hunt bolting across, and Buse and Virgie would return early with the little shaggy pony at the point of exhaustion. From an upstairs window Toots, feigning a headache and sore throat, watched them leave. She clutched her robe to her chest and bit her lip.

They trotted in single file down dirt roads through stands of trees hard and leafless for winter. The talking and laughter faded. Far ahead the hounds yelped and howled, Harold blew long, lyrical blasts on his horn, and Majestic, head of the pack, bayed in return. They fanned out onto rough fields, the dogs had the scent, a fox well known in the area was on the run. The horses were strung out, up they went over fences of stone and wood, riders and animals perspired in the cold air. Someone fell.

Michael held Turf to the rear, he avoided getting in the way of riders more experienced than himself. Far off he saw Buse and Virgie sitting still and watching. The hunt was a rainbow that curved, blanketed a field, broke into chips of bright color, disappeared. Turf was obedient, he cleared the ditches and fences with room to spare. The horse was like a gentle roller coaster as Harry and Uncle Harold had said, never had Michael felt such a long, slow motion in the gallop. He heard a cry. He watched as not a hundred yards to his left a horse that had shied at a fence and thrown his rider, an elderly woman who was a fortepiano player and friend of Aunt Alexandra, suddenly reared and brought his front hooves crashing down on the woman's thighs. Again, and the inexplicably crazed animal tossed his head, reins flying, and charged into a nearby wood. Michael pulled on Turf, but already a crowd of men had leapt to the ground and were kneeling, surrounding her. He rode on, shivering, feeling suddenly cold, and still he heard the thud of her body, the horse's squeal, the unthinkable silence of the hooves coming down on the woman. For the first time in his life he was giddy. Before he knew it, the fence was ahead of him, high and smothered in a tangle of briars, and he had just time to recover, to collect Turf, to guide him up so the horizon fell away and at the crest they were suspended at this unexpected height before going down. Michael was low and forward in the jumping position, he stared straight out and away over Turf's head with the air caught in his mouth, his eyes watering, and despite what had happened to the woman and his being alone—it came to him that there was not another rider in sight—he knew he still had the big bay in hand and felt the tingling sensation of being at the crest of a dangerously high jump.

But Turf stumbled—not badly—when landing. It was enough. Michael fell slightly forward, gasped, allowed his cold hands to slide to either side of the plaited mane—Turf's mane was plaited with red and green ribbons—and in that moment he lost everything. Turf took the bit in his teeth, veered to the right toward the distant outbuildings of a small farm bordering this empty field, and thundered off as if Michael had already fallen and the great bay were free. Gone the roller-coaster action. Shattered the lulling sensations of sitting forward atop the horse. No longer was there anything familiar about the working muscles, the hooves striking the hard ground in the tremendous flat-out gallop. Nor were the ears back and flattened to the skull, as was usually the case with the runaway horse giving vent to the mean spirit behind the bold surprise, the act of defiance. If anything, his ears were more forward than Michael was used to seeing them on Turf's proud head, the lathered animal racing only in his most enthusiastic mood.

There might have been a crowd cheering. Turf was winning as he usually did. But there was no crowd. Only the empty field, blue-colored, the sound of the hooves on the frozen earth, and Michael wobbling from side to side. He could not breathe. Turf's neck was almost horizontal with his body. Again he veered. And suddenly the outbuildings of the little Pytchley farm were near and horse and helpless rider were closing in on them with amazing speed and suddenly obvious intent. Michael could not turn the horse, he did not try. A milk shed, its roof sloping flatly down in their direction to within two or three feet of the ground, separated itself from the rest. There it was, directly in their path, unavoidable. Had Turf taken it into his head to smash them into Mr. Pytchley's milking shed? In all his raging playfulness he would destroy them both!

For one instant Michael considered flinging himself off before they struck, but in the next the shed loomed before them and Turf jumped. Up he went, landing in mid-roof, and the violent hooves did not crash through the planking, he lost not a stride. Michael heard a loud cry—Mr. Pytchley's wife was below, inside, milking the cows—and up went Turf, bounding toward the high edge of the roof, empty sky and a filigree of dead treetops far in the distance. Michael hung on. The mad ride had not ended in disaster and a loud massive splintering of wood. But only one thing was left. Turf was going to jump from the top of the roof!

Again there was only a moment in which he could hear the clean and dreadful clatter of hooves and the enormous bay preparing his haunches, starting the engine of his great hindquarters, and then they were at the lip of that flat roof and Turf leapt away. Off and out they sailed. Michael clung for his life. Through the silence they sailed, straight out from the edge of the roof, and down below Mr. Pytchley's wife looked up at them, face white and jaws slack, and began shouting something Michael could not hear in the cold sibilance of the highest and longest jump made by any member in the collective memory of the Van Fleet Hunt.

They began their descent, smaller sheds and a manure pile and a hay wagon flying up to meet them. They struck, they thundered to earth, they crashed through a pile of milking tins and with hardly a thought jumped the hay wagon. Then a fence—it was nothing—another open field. On they went without one pause, one lost stride, one change in direction. And still Michael stayed on. What, if anything, would shake him loose? Fall he must, it was inevitable, and he longed to be done with it. In no way did Turf show any signs of his exertions except for the flecks of foam flying back from the captive bit and the dark growing stains of sweat that Michael now and then saw and felt. What would stop him? Would he never slow down? Would he shake Michael loose without meaning to do so and then trip over the slightest obstacle and crash to earth himself? Or would they go down together? Or would Turf flay them both in the stand of black trees far ahead?

Michael felt a jolt, a mere ripple of unexpected motion.

They had jumped a ditch that he had not even seen. And over he began to go at last. He gave up. He flung away the reins, he lost his left stirrup and his left foot rose, the stirrup flew, he slid to the right, feared that his right foot, which was still caught in the stirrup, would not come free. There he would hang, twisting and turning high from the flashing ground, victim of Turf's terrible hooves.

He was stretched out straight from Turf's right side. His left calf lay across the saddle, his right foot was free. But he did not fall. Could not fall. On they went at the same speed and there he was, suspended. Impossibly suspended. Attached to the horse by nothing more than his left leg. He caught a glimpse of two riders approaching from the far right, one in black coat, one in red. Too distant to help but not too distant to see him, no matter how small the image, floundering in this ignoble position. They were waving, he lost sight of them. He was facing forward in the direction of Turf's dark head—the handsome, brutal head alive with passion—and thought with despair that he was not the horseman Uncle Harold and Harry Martin had judged him to be. If the horse were injured, it would be his fault. Then it was that the great head began to swing to the right, to turn, until Turf's enormous glistening amber-colored eyes were full upon him. Never had Turf seen anything like it, his rider hanging in the rushing air beside him, and in a burst of disdain—not panic surely—surged forward faster than ever. Michael felt the speed, felt himself dislodged at last. Down he went.

His first hunt. His first hunting accident. His first broken bones. When he awoke in the warmth and softness of his own bed at Steepleton, Uncle Harold and Aunt Alexandra on his right side and the doctor on his left, he savored immediately the timeless pleasures of the young and injured. Uncle Harold and Aunt Alexandra looked alike in their boots and britches and white shirts, yellow vests, white stocks, still dressed for the hunt except for their coats, the one pink and the other black, which they had flung on a chair beside his bed. The Master of Foxhounds towered above his wife head and shoulders, but together their faces were drawn and white for Michael's sake. And it did not matter that they had brought the smells of fox and horse into the decorum of his room. Only his well-being mattered. The doctor had his sleeves rolled up. Michael smelled the delicious scent of medicinal alcohol. Turf had not suffered a scratch, Uncle Harold said, though the big bay had given them a merry chase.

Only weeks later, long after the hunting season was over, Michael learned that Toots and not himself had been the true victim of that grim day. Aunt Alexandra sat beside him on the edge of his bed and entertained him with books from the library downstairs and brought his meals on a tray herself. But weeks later, no matter how well he was beginning to feel, Steepleton had not yet recovered, and his injuries were hardly enough to account for the change in the family's mood. It came back to him—the sounds of weeping and someone running, the low voices far into the night, the unexpected sound of a car engine. Aunt Alexandra continued to be red-eyed when she brought the tray or a heavy book, and was unaware of Virgie listening in Michael's doorway. Uncle Harold's face was still as drawn and white as hers.

Finally, one late afternoon, Aunt Alexandra led him to understand that all this sorrow was not for himself but Toots. Uncle Harold had been the one who had found her dead on the very day of Michael's fall. She was gone for good. After that afternoon neither Uncle Harold nor Aunt Alexandra ever spoke of Toots again. Even Virgie learned not to ask for her sister but instead stayed as close to Michael as she could.

Michael recovered, Uncle Harold gave him a frisky but well-mannered liver-colored horse named Cripple, after a famous horse of the past, saying he had outgrown Chuckers, and they worked long hours together in the ring while Virgie sat alone in the bleachers and watched. It was at this time, after Michael's injury and Toots's death, that Michael's help was enlisted to lace the corset. Time and again Uncle Harold said that if he had acquired his "back," as he called it, in a fall like Michael's, he would have been proud.

* * *

*If you can't hold your horse, go home. There is nothing more
dangerous in the hunt field than a horse out of control. He risks not
only his rider's neck but also the necks of everyone else in the field.
The purpose of fox hunting is only this: to seek out, chase, and kill a
fox with a pack of foxhounds. Don't take any more jumps than you
have to. Keep your eyes open. Don't speak during the check when
the hounds are working. Don't cut in on the horse ahead of you.
Defer to the Master.*

What happened to Hal?

II

THE
HORSE PAINTER

THE SOUL OF the Van Fleet family was aesthetic. It was not a mystery, it had its source.

The wiry little Walter T. Van Fleet may have worn his long johns summer and winter and dressed himself tightly and solemnly in black suit and high white collar even in the modern day of Michael's youth, which he did, and in his person and taciturnity belied anything like the aesthetic sensibility. To most it appeared that he was interested only in horses. But Grandfather's love of the horse purebred or not was based on an aesthetic knowledge and passion which few suspected but which had come to him, man to boy, from his own father and in similar fashion had been passed on to Grandfather's own son. Old John Van Fleet had spent his life acquiring and contemplating works of art, including masterpieces, as Walter used to say and after him Harold, and imitations. And in certain cases the copies were more enticing than the originals. Walter was as aware as any connoisseur of the curious limitations of Old John's taste, which was confined to representations of women, usually of the frolicking or surrendering sort, and of horses. On certain days the old man, far taller and more severe than Grandfather had become, preferred his women while on certain days he favored the horses. But the horses prevailed. At Steepleton the canvases of Great-Grandfather's collection had gathered in every corner, hung on every wall. Great-Grandmother had objected to the life-sized women in shining pinks and pale blues displaying themselves on swings and cushions, so most of the walls finally went to horses and most of the corners to the joyous, languorous women. There were not many paintings left at Steepleton by the time of Michael's boyhood, but there were enough.

Whistlejacket, the immense cream- and coffee-colored stallion rearing up as if under the promptings of an invisible rider—there was no human figure in the painting, no background or saddle and bridle—remained the only work of art in Steepleton's grand salon, except for a rustic scene above the fireplace. Along with the fortepiano it appeared to fill the room that was so large that once in the eccentric past of the Van Fleet family, long before the advent of Aunt Alexandra's fortepiano, Old John had brought his Whips, all five of them still mounted like himself and fresh from the hunt, clomping into the grand salon to admire Whistlejacket, one of the finest portraits of a horse ever painted by George Stubbs. The horses of the five Whips trod on polished floors and French floor coverings, the men said down to a man that looking at Whistlejacket from the saddle gave a new and admirable perspective to the grandeur of the horse, no matter that several of the living horses shied from the painted animal or attempted to rear up in imitation of it. This event sent Great-Grandmother to her bed for a week.

The east wall of the dining salon, a vast beamed and tiled room in the Renaissance style, was dominated by Whistlejacket's counterpart, a portrait of a sleeping woman. She lay flushed of face in her rumpled bed while beside her stood a suited man—her husband—holding a letter which but moments before he had snatched up from the feathery bed. The angered face of the husband contrasted magnificently, Grandfather had said, with the round, contented face of the woman, which looked as if it had been rendered in the creamiest of white and rose enamels. This painting, Grandfather pointed out many a time, was the work of an unknown painter. But an artist who knew his women and colors and brushstrokes well.

Grandfather was proud of what he had learned about art. He was proud of his special gift of sight. At the peak of his professional career he was amused that his ability to recognize the true identity of a disguised horse, no matter how skillfully the horse's markings and colorings had been changed through the use of dyes, depended on his aesthetic eye. He was proud that he had been his father's student. And like his father, the artist he most admired, the one who had filled his boyhood with exhilaration, was not a famous painter of lively women but rather the modest horse painter George Stubbs. Grandfather never forgot what his own father had said: that Stubbs was the first to see beneath the skin to the flesh and bone of the horse.

Early in his life Stubbs discovered for himself two simple laws, which were never to paint from anything but nature and never to paint what he saw from the outside unless he had seen the inside first. At the age of five he began to draw and soon he was dissecting cats and dogs for the sake of his art. In young manhood this tanner's son anatomized human cadavers and dead horses for love of the living bodies he painted. After Stubbs, Grandfather said, no horse was ever shown again in impossible postures.

The boy is deceptively the man. Some men are born already old, as they say. But in some men, who look fully grown when they are small, the boys they really were for a time are not extinguished by manhood. Rather than the child's being the father of the man, the grown man remains a boy. The boy's sway grows as youth and then maturity appear. The boy thrives. The larger the body he inhabits, the more that adult experience accumulates around him, the more that this man commands respect and power, then the more the secret boy consumes, discards, acquires only what he wants for his own purposes and needs to ensure the man's veneer. The boy lives on inside the man. This man is innocent, inventive, dogged. He gets his own way.

Such a man, such a boy was George Stubbs, horse painter. He weighed thirteen pounds at birth. By the age of two years, when he was an indefatigable walker and could concentrate for long hours on any task he considered profitable to himself, he was already physically formed into the man he would shortly appear to be. Large and weighty, face shaped into a mask of sensual porcine features, bland eyes that seemed to see too much, arms too strong for his size. He was agreeable and obedient, up to a point.

By the age of seven he was at work in his father's tannery in Hull, England, was leader of a group of boys adept at capturing cats and dogs for dissection, and was already so accomplished a draftsman that his father rightly feared that his favorite son, George, would not spend his life as an accomplished tanner and the proprietor of the family enterprise. When dissecting cats and mongrels, the painter-to-be was not avid, cruel, aimless as were many of the other boys, but was methodical, intent, paring away the wretched creatures until the bones gleamed and the various small organs stirred in him the longing to inspect much larger ones.

It appeared that he could not improve his drawing, he had learned all he could about the tanning trade. Still he was patient and remained in his father's prosperous works until at last Stubbs senior died, willing the tannery not to his favorite son but to his wife. George Stubbs, taken to be a grown man by most, was sixteen years old. He left Hull, attached himself as a pupil-helper to a painter in the north, quarreled with that mediocre portraitist, and returned to Hull, where, supported by his mother, he taught himself the skills of applying paint to canvas.

Satisfied with himself but nagged by a need he associated with the sick and dying, he left his mother and found employment in the St. Bartholomew Hospital at York. He served the dying, handled corpses, attended lectures in anatomy, and became the closest friend of the most vivid lecturer in those drafty halls, the eminent young surgeon Charles Atkinson. The two were of similar age and the slight, good-humored Atkinson knew at once that in his pouting, heavyset companion he had found a man as determined as himself to expose the secret machinery of the human body and to delight in the internal organs no matter their degree of putrefaction.

As soon as Stubbs met Atkinson, the others appeared. Mary Spencer, who one afternoon with mop and pail in a corridor of the hospital raised her head and showed Stubbs an expression he could not deny. Lord and Lady Nelthorpe—John and Sophia—who lived near York in Colwick Hall in Barton and, though even younger than Stubbs and Atkinson, were already the parents of a son whose visage was a perfect likeness of Stubbs's own. Dr. William Smellie, chief of surgery at St. Bartholomew. Plain but devoted Mary Spencer, a sweet woman of erotic candor that contrasted surprisingly with her otherwise self-effacing manner, soon after their meeting became Stubbs's common-law wife for the rest of his days. John Nelthorpe the child, a spoiled boy whom Lady Nelthorpe entertained each day as if he were a man or she herself were a child, broke his arm and leg in a fall from his pony, and it was Atkinson who repaired the thankless boy and introduced his friend George Stubbs to the mother. Before the week was out, Lady Nelthorpe became Stubbs's first patron, commissioning him to paint her son's portrait at Colwick Hall, with promises of more work to come. Dr. Smellie, a little man capable of the most vulgar language and the greatest rages ever known in the hospital in York, and whose wife had just borne him a son in her middle years—a son who survived—was obsessed with preparing a study of midwifery that would be the first such book to appear. Smellie had taken an interest in Stubbs when Atkinson had introduced the two. Smellie could make no progress on his midwifery project without the anatomization of a woman who had died before her infant could be born and without an artist to draw and then engrave the plates showing the dissected womb containing its lifeless child. Smellie, without good reason to do so, decided that Stubbs could both find and dissect the subject and prepare the plates.

One late afternoon when the last of the students had left the hall, Atkinson, still glistening with the sweat of his brilliance, stayed on, signaling his friend Stubbs to do the same. It was cold, Stubbs remained where he was, bundled in heavy coat and frayed sweater, hunched over the long, narrow bench carved with the initials and crude designs of former students. Charles joined him, sat atop the bench on which the students on either side of Stubbs had been resting their heads in sleep—even a lecturer like Atkinson could not hold the attention of all. Charles's stained white coat hung open, its skirts swung down, his shirt was wet, but obviously he did not feel the cold.

In an animated, furtive voice Charles told his friend that he had news. George waited. Charles waited as well for effect. Then Charles told George that an old farmer's young wife had died and was still aboveground only sixteen miles away. George remained impassive, Charles became more excited and spoke in tones hardly more than a whisper. The point, Charles said, was that this dead woman had been in her eighth month of pregnancy. George's lips formed what Charles considered to be an endearing pout. The woman, George said, would soon be buried, and furthermore, Lady Nelthorpe had already commissioned him to paint her son. George waited. Charles smiled. Do both, he told his friend. George was silent, forcing his agitated friend to be explicit. Charles said that George must both anatomize the woman and paint the boy.

George opened his heavy lips, then shut them and said that Lady Nelthorpe had invited him to stay at Colwick Hall. As if clapping George on the shoulder, Charles said that the farm where the young woman lay was sixteen miles from York but only two from Barton. Farm and manor house were situated in the same small circle of earth and air. George had only to persuade Lady Nelthorpe that he could not accept her hospitality since for the sake of science he must spend his nights in York, but from York to Barton was an easy ride. The cadaver of the old farmer's wife could easily be bought, especially if they rented the farm itself and sent the desperate man to recuperate in York. For two weeks George and Mary Spencer would live on the farm while George painted the portrait of the young Lord Nelthorpe in the daylight hours and dissected the cadaver of the pregnant woman in the dark nights.

George considered the plan. Slowly the forces of his determination gathered. He agreed. The future of his art was guaranteed. There with the prospect of exploring the rare body of the woman before him—the most fortunate of opportunities since at the time the procuring of any cadaver other than that of the criminal was a vile and unlawful act— he was already forming his notions of a monumental study of the horse.

Lady Nelthorpe did not believe George Stubbs when he presented his plan, thinking that he must have discovered some young married woman in York, perhaps one he had been asked to sketch by her dull-witted husband. But she smiled, pleased at the thought of her newfound portraitist putting aside his brushes and palette for the arms of a rosy wife who had piqued his taste, and said she understood and that Colwick Hall was ready and waiting if he should change his mind. They set the dates for her son's sittings.

Colwick Hall by day, the farm by nights. Atkinson supplied the medical provender and in a carriage with drawn shades brought to the Dyer farm everything that Stubbs would need: rubber sheets, rubber gloves and apron, rubber tubing, dusty bottles of the indispensable carbolic acid, along with the flat wooden cases containing a full array of the knives and scissors and clamps that shone in the light. He left in high spirits and apprehension, glancing once over his shoulder at the long, low cottage with its gray stone walls and a roof that had already lost a dismaying portion of its sodden thatch.

Stubbs and Mary Spencer decided not to remove Mary Dyer—they did not speak of the irony of her name—from the bed where she had conceived and died in the farmer's crude sleeping chamber at the far end of the cottage. Winter was just giving way to spring, they hoped for continuing cold days and heavy frosts at night. They shuttered every window, hung an extra blanket over the closed door to the room where Mary Dyer lay, built only the smallest fires in the soot-blackened kitchen, and took the little sleep they allowed themselves in what was no more than an empty storage space with a stone floor. But this room of sorts was at the opposite end of the cottage from Mary Dyer.

The few animals remaining on the farm withdrew as far as

they could into the fallow lands beyond the cottage, Stubbs's own horse—a sturdy, good-tempered cob with a docked tail—tried repeatedly to escape from the barn. Even returning birds suddenly changed course and veered around the Dyer farm, vanished from sight. There was not a fresh breeze to be felt.

As usual since they had arrived, Mary Spencer scrubbed Stubbs's naked tallowlike flesh from top to bottom just at sunrise. The water from the bucket burned her hands, she shivered, she lathered the impassive man with the cake of yellow soap, swung the bucket. She did not complain as she had not complained for all the hours she had stood beside him already in the light of candles clustered unnaturally around the bed and room, just as she did not complain when not long after, her ordeal worsened. She assisted him, wondering how any woman who wanted to bear children could stand by and watch and listen and obey her husband while, as slowly as a yellow slug chewing a leaf, he anatomized Mary Dyer. Her only concession was, each night, to wrap a long strip of linen around her nose and mouth. Stubbs worked with uncovered face and even bare hands, ignoring the rubber gloves which she coveted but would not even suggest that she wear. Once when she asked him timorously if he did not find it hard to breathe, he merely raised himself slightly from his stooped position, stared at her slowly with his honey-colored eyes, and shook his head. The tiers of candles gleamed, the broad slope of his forehead was dry and shone in the light.

For half the night they stood over the body, for the other half he made sketches, and then at the wooden table where Mary Dyer had served her husband his meals, he sat hunched over the drawings that would become the plates in Dr. Smellie's *Midwifery Book*. Finally, with two hours left until sunrise, she begged him to sleep and together they retired to their storeroom and makeshift bed of straw and stiff blankets.

She marveled that he did not shiver or look the least bit weary when the shard of red light shattered on the horizon and she washed him down just as, she once thought with a silent giggle, he washed down his horse.

No matter whether the new day was gray or bright, moist in a thaw or thinly virginal in one of the last powderings of snow, and no matter whether Stubbs had managed two hours or three of sleep, he always set off for Colwick Hall with the same vigor, hardly to be detected, that he brought to the time when he could again take up the knife or pencil in the Dyer cottage. Once mounted on his dark cob, Jeffrey, Stubbs saw that the Dyer cottage was only a dismal place to leave as quickly as possible, and when the day was over at Colwick Hall, the Dyer cottage was again inviting, though it looked abandoned when he arrived back at dusk. Colwick Hall stood in its park, a long, low, handsome building of brick, and it was the promised hospitality of the place that at first kept him on guard in the midst of pleasure.

He worked in a small parlor warmed and lit by a coal fire and made openly feminine by walls and ceiling covered in damask of a rich green sweetened with yellow. Velvet drapes matched the color of the walls and ceiling. The fire glowed, fresh roses from the greenhouse adorned the mantel in a white vase. His easel was inevitably in place, brushes and tubes of paint and palette laid out and waiting. The single chair near the small fireplace was not for the odd-shaped little boy but his mother.

The child refused to remain in the pretty parlor alone with Stubbs, which necessitated the mother. Furthermore, the young Lord Nelthorpe could not stand still unless he stood beside his seated mother—Sophia—and kept a hand on her shoulder. Stubbs and Sophia deceived the boy into thinking that this oil painting would portray the two of them, mother and son. Whereas Stubbs and Lady Nelthorpe had agreed from the start that Stubbs would paint her out of the portrait once it was completed and the boy had lost interest.

Day by careful day Stubbs worked at his easel, creating the splendid boy on canvas while the true posing was done by the mother. The more time Stubbs spent painting her child, the clearer it became that Sophia was his subject, or wanted to be, and that her actual wish was to remain alone in the portrait, her son and not herself obliterated by the heavy polished hand holding the brush.

The boy fretted, the mother did not move. Yet it was the

boy who demanded silence, perhaps to listen for his heavy-set father riding home with the hounds, and more than once told his mother sharply that she must not speak. The boy was seven, the mother, twenty-four.

Stubbs turned the curl of the lips to agreeableness and made the little top-heavy body proportionate by lengthening the legs. He thinned the hair, made the face less weighty, tightened the calves, and added shadows so that the boy's legs were of the shape and age of a diminutive man's. The clothes of the young John Nelthorpe had been chosen for the sitting by the mother, and chosen so well, reflected Stubbs, that on certain days it seemed that she was the secret artist and he merely her draftsman. The living figures before him were positioned so that the boy's right hand was resting on his mother's shoulder while her right forearm rested on the gilt arm of the chair with her slender hand pointing downwards. The boy's right knee was bent, his left arm bent at the elbow, his little hand casually propped on his hip, and his weight supported by his left side. He might have been a small patrician posing with his hand on the head of a whippet against a background of dark late-summer clouds.

Lady Nelthorpe asked if he was doing justice to her son. The child rebuked his mother. Stubbs reassured Lady Nelthorpe, who he knew was confident enough of his abilities. She smiled. She asked him if he ever took such delight in his work that he wanted to touch the fresh paint with his fingers. Did he ever wish to smear the canvas merely to feel the wet strokes he himself had applied? The boy stamped his foot, Stubbs turned and looked at her while his hand and fingers continued their magical moving apparently without the need of his eyes. Lady Nelthorpe declared that as a girl she had been tutored in watercoloring and regretted that she had had no talent. Stubbs answered, though he rarely spoke at Colwick Hall, saying that at times it was better to be the artist's subject than the artist. The young Lord Nelthorpe left the room. Lady Nelthorpe said she had angered him. They heard Lord Nelthorpe the father riding into the stableyard with his Whips and friends. Stubbs covered the painting, cleaned his brushes. She rose, stood at his side. Soon, she said, the painting would be finished.

So too, he told Jeffrey, would his work on Mary Dyer and her unborn, unnamed son. And to think, he told Jeffrey, that it took as long to draw the head of the lifeless infant as it did to paint the entire trim on the knee-length waistcoat of the boy, as long to draw one of the lifeless legs of the infant as to paint the overly large tapering fingers of the boy's right hand. Thick as a grapevine—Stubbs was incapable of sentimentalizing his horse but talked to him anyway—and looking more like a gnarled vine in a wintry field than like the supple length of physiological tubing he had expected, the umbilical cord alone took hours. Two grand projects, Stubbs said as the Dyer cottage came into sight and Jeffrey picked up his heavy trot. Two artistic projects impossible to choose from since the one would further his career as much as the other.

Despite their need for secrecy, Mary Spencer increasingly opened the shutters in his absence. She could not help herself. Crows were gathering. There was always a faint line of smoke ascending from the chimney of the darkened cottage to greet his return each evening, always the smell of strong soap and cold water to accompany him each morning as he set off for Colwick Hall. By mid-ride Lady Nelthorpe's scent inevitably sprang from the wet spring countryside, an icy sweetness as faint as the flowers beneath the snow, an aroma he recognized with every new turn in the road.

There came the day when Stubbs spent longer at his easel than he had meant to. The temperature had fallen in the midst of a thaw, the tips of new shoots were shrouded in a glaze of ice, the entire day had been clear and fresh, spring itself lay frozen for miles around Colwick Hall while the light of the cold sun shone against the blue of the sky and struck the tenderest of icicles from the limbs of trees and eaves of the stables. But all day the light that had filled the intimate green of the parlor had been of a soft orange warmth in color. A last ray, broad and aimed at a slant through the thin glass as if intentionally at Lady Nelthorpe, had fallen upon her seated figure and for an hour or more caused the colors of her gown to brighten like the soft coals in the grate behind her. The gown she wore was of a floral pattern, pinkish ivory flowers and orange flowers, each as large as the painter's fist, floating in the creamy taffeta folds of her gown—though Lady Nelthorpe herself sat perfectly still and upright in her chair, hand dangling as usual, eyes upon him, smiling. The boy too had commented on the beauty of the flower-patterned gown.

Stubbs took a step back from the easel, suddenly more interested in the full-length figure he had painted than in the woman he had been watching while painting her son. At this moment even Lady Nelthorpe and her floral gown, which was unlike any he had ever seen, were nothing compared with the young boy who stared back at Stubbs from the canvas. What, he asked himself, had he done? The auburn hair—like the mother's but of a darker shade—and the golden beige of the knee-length coat, the burnt red that tinged the muddied gold of the lower portion of the waistcoat and its broad trim, the beige and ivory mass of the waistcoat that was wrinkled and shadowed by the plumpness of the boy's torso, and the ivory ruffles that bound the throat and the dark brown satin of the britches concealing his little legs to below the knee, all of this figure displayed in the spring green parlor like a gem in its setting—what loveliness, Stubbs asked himself, had he fashioned in this way to last forever? The child's face mirrored the father's, Stubbs told himself, not the mother's. The dimples, the fleshy lips, the large forehead, the dark, undiscerning eyes. The father, of course, the dull-witted father. Never could Stubbs have brought himself to portray this boy as revealing any trait at all of the mother.

He moved still farther from his painting, brush held to the side, not in a dramatic gesture but only to restrain its tip from the canvas. Nothing in this portrait of the young Lord Nelthorpe allowed for change. Nothing. Stubbs had brought the boy from bone and soul to finished figure. In days, a week, a month, years ahead, the surfaces and depths of this work would still shine as now when the paint was fresh. He decided that it did not need his signature.

Finished, whispered the seated woman in obvious pleasure, finished. Stubbs nodded. The boy stepped forward, inspected the work, declared this rendering of his mother passable and that the work should hang at the end of the entranceway of Colwick Hall, and left the room. Stubbs waited. Would not Lady Nelthorpe also stand beside him for her first glimpse of the completed portrait? But no, she was still in her chair. Awkwardly Stubbs set down his brush, his palette, glanced again at his modest triumph, turned toward the woman, admitting to himself that the gown she wore was more handsome than the pale silver-colored gown in the painting. And the woman who was teasing him with her silence wore no jewelry while in the painting there was the thinnest diamond choker around her throat. The throat without adornment was preferable. Precisely as Stubbs made this comparison, and as there came the boyish noises of the sportsmen once again leaving the stableyard to silence, the hands, only the hands, moved. In all his physical bulk and poor posture, Stubbs watched, concentrated, memorized what he was about to see. He glanced at her clever face, stared at the hands. Slowly the fingers took hold of the taffeta at the knees, the hemline of the abundant gown began to rise, the ankles, the lower calves came into view. No further covering of any kind concealed what she was exposing. The shaft of sunlight in which she sat was so firm, so clear, so warm that neither one of them would be able to speak as long as it turned one side of Lady Nelthorpe into brightness and caused dark shadows to smudge the other. Her feet and lower legs were extended slightly toward the edge of the light. There might have been silent children playing about her feet. But already she had destroyed the last vestige of domesticity. Up rose the hem of the skirt, slowly, he saw the knees—the small, shiny knees—and still she continued to bare herself, drawing the gathered taffeta to mid-thigh, and the light remained constant. He watched, waited, the expression on her heart-shaped face began to change. The hands, the gathered taffeta held between the tips of the fingers ceased to move. Her bare legs were fully exposed to this man.

Behind her a single round coal that had thoroughly consumed itself and become a perfect mass of crystalline heat slipped from its place on the burning heap, fell a small distance, and shattered with a rustling feathery sound on the bed of embers.

For an hour following sunset Stubbs painted the figure of Sophia Nelthorpe out of the portrait as agreed. She did not look at the painting until Stubbs said there was nothing left of herself to see.

Mary Spencer knew that Stubbs had completed his first commission at Colwick Hall the moment she greeted him in the swampy yard behind the cottage. Even before he dismounted he told her—the Nelthorpe painting was done. And within the hour, Mary Spencer knew, she would spend no more time in the room with Mary Dyer. Only another night or two of cold stones, blankets she could hardly bring herself to turn down, and the smell of the gases that flow from the unburied dead.

Mary Spencer could no longer share the nightly meal she prepared for Stubbs. However, she thought with a smile, it did not matter. She cleared the table more important to him for drawing than eating, he described his portrait of the Nelthorpe heir, they went as they always did to Mary Dyer's room. The more candles they lit, the more shadows gathered in the room and around the bed like charred portions of the air itself. Mary Spencer wrapped her nose and mouth in her cloth, she reminded Stubbs to wear the long surgical coat, once white. The anatomization of Mary Dyer was all but complete and, to Mary Spencer, had even been carried to unnecessary lengths, Stubbs having satisfied himself as to the full situation of the enlarged uterus, its relationship to the stomach and its compressing effect within the body as high as the lungs; he knew which veins and arteries were fullest and what distortions had been imposed on the bladder; he showed Mary Spencer that the kidneys were oversize, as was the heart. But it was the infant she cared most about, the infant he studied, going so far as to seize it and turn it this way and that in the uterine space whose elasticity conformed to the infant's every impatient move. Candles burned out, light jumped and stuttered across what was now the shimmering formlessness of Mary Dyer's remains. Stubbs peered down, cut something, spent a moment with his sketchpad, then declared himself done with the cadaver. He straightened, waited for Mary Spencer to pinch out the last of the candles, which she did in haste, admitting to herself that no ordinary dignity could be restored to Mary Dyer and that her removal from the cottage must be left to obliging medical students as planned by Stubbs and Charles Atkinson.

Once again Stubbs sat at the table and stooped his shoulders so that, as always, he worked in his own shadow. But he was diligent, determined, and the final diagrammatic drawing of the infant grew. She arranged fresh candles around him as best she could, watched, seeing little, sat across from him wrapped in a blanket. She did not allow herself to sleep. She was needed, she knew, and waited. She heard the mice, heard the cold air creaking above in the beams. Could conditions be any worse for an artist? Yet he was smiling.

Toward dawn Stubbs put down his pencil, leaned back, flexed his fingers. He was finished. And it was then that Mary Spencer had her reward, since at that moment, without a pause, Stubbs said she must see his exhibition, and without stretching his shoulders or stifling a yawn, he spread out the sixteen drawings for her to see. He stood beside her, settling his large size close to her sparse smallness, and in his familiar expectant silence waited as she began to look. She could feel his full pleasure, so rarely evident, the sheer bulk and power of this man obviously immune to the cold. She looked. She bent closer to study the large drawings flat on the table. She too began to smile. How, she asked herself, had he been able to transform the shapes and surfaces which to her had become increasingly indistinct into these anatomically exact—she was convinced that they must be anatomically exact—reproductions of the infant on the eve of its birth while at the same time giving the image—the infant—a determined little life of its own? Why, she thought, no other infant at the time of birth had looked like this one, none but this one could have weighed so much or taken such possession of the womb in which it was both confined and sustained. These were correct drawings but surely not clinical drawings, she thought, since Stubbs had shaded with fine cross-hatching both womb and child. And what had he made of Mary Dyer's infant? Nothing less than a chubby acrobat. Here he was curled up in peace but not symmetrically since even here, in what must be the easiest posture for the unborn infant to assume, one small fat leg was bent down, creating a counterangle to the other leg, which, upraised, concealed one of the little forearms. And here he was the swimmer or perhaps the diver bent backwards on his stomach in the womb that was his, and even the fingers were plain to see—his fist was clenched!—the toes of the two feet as distinctly drawn as the hand. Oh, but it was an awkward position that he could not keep for long.

Mary Spencer straightened, smiled up into the heavy face, then returned to the drawings. She chose her favorite two: in the first he had gotten himself upside down and was holding his elbows to his sides and resting on his nearly square head, which actually distended the womb downwards as if he were already beginning his struggle into the air. The fat little buttocks were high, making two healthy curves, and again the symmetry was broken by one rebellious thigh that jutted out to one side and the leg and foot—a single foot!—thrust into the crosshatched darkness slightly above the buttocks. Here the spine was nothing but a few dots in a vertical row, yet she found herself wanting to run a finger down the bones beneath the fat. Lastly he was on his back, one plump leg hiding the other, but here—and best of all to see—he was driving one arm straight out to the side, sheathing his violent arm in the elastic wall. A little undaunted man, she thought, a sturdy little man even before he was born. But why, suddenly, did he seem so familiar? She puzzled a moment, gave up, accepted the drawings for themselves only, and then turning and embracing her Stubbs, whispered that he was nothing less than a master.

The *Midwifery Book* was widely hailed. Whenever he returned from a visit to Lady Nelthorpe, Charles Atkinson was as happily animated as Stubbs was noncommittal over the success that Stubbs had obviously made of himself at Colwick Hall.

Stubbs was not surprised when one day Atkinson returned with the second invitation from Lady Nelthorpe— to paint her and Lord Nelthorpe posing together on horseback. Stubbs knew at once that the discreet inclusion of the husband was the wife's doing but that the inclusion of the horses came from the husband. And thanks to John Nelthorpe—not his wife—the subject that had been waiting to absorb Stubbs all the while he had lived at the Dyer cottage and during his many weeks back in York stood before him—the horse. Only the complete anatomy of the horse would do. How else to paint faithfully the creature that Stubbs loved most?

So again Stubbs visited Lady Nelthorpe, speaking to her in such a way that she became his patroness not only for the present and future paintings but also for the project—he could not describe it fully, he confessed—that was consuming him. Lady Nelthorpe bore well the impersonal conversation, colored somewhat, but then was privately amused that Stubbs, as he told her in passing, had married. As his patroness, she said, she would do all and everything he asked.

The average horse of the time weighed perhaps twelve hundred pounds. Such a horse was the equivalent in weight to six or eight men, and the top of its head was all but beyond the reach of the upstretched arm of Mary Spencer. And this was the creature Stubbs meant to anatomize as he had the cadaver of Mary Dyer? Furthermore, as Stubbs began to make increasingly clear, he planned to undertake this dissection with an attention to minutiae he had not even attempted to devote to the dead woman. Section by section, part by part from the largest to the smallest, Stubbs intended to expose all there was to expose of the horse. In the end there would be nothing left except the skeleton. He could go no further than the skeleton, Stubbs told Mary Spencer, and he intended to articulate the skeleton. She would see. And so she should, she thought, yet how could he do it? Where would he find the horses—for she knew at his first words that a single horse would not suffice—and where would the laborious dissections be performed, and how was he to handle animals so large, so heavy? Who would help him? Even as she asked the question, she became resigned. Ahead of her she saw stretching more paths of blood, more nights of fright, more secrecy, more impossible work than she could bear. Surely Mary Dyer had been enough. But there was no alternative. Hers would be the willingness Stubbs expected. Nothing less.

A few miles outside Harkstow, a village nine miles from Colwick Hall instead of two, but as much under the aegis of Lady Nelthorpe as Barton was, a tenant farm presented itself for his use. The main cottage was clean and dry with a well-thatched roof and kind furnishings. More important, the monumental work they would soon begin was to be done not in the cottage but in a sturdy windowless outbuilding in which the overhead beams were massive and the floor was of stone. In Harkstow Stubbs readily found tallow, rope, candles, pulleys, chain, iron rods, hammers and wrenches, planking, and a blacksmith's forge along with the coal it required. Again Charles Atkinson provided the surgeon's instruments without which Stubbs could not proceed to lay bare the horse for scientist, artist, and ordinary horseman to see and profit by.

Together in the cold outbuilding—late fall brought fog, rain, sudden brightening of sun and air—Stubbs and Mary Spencer contemplated how to manage the carcasses of the horses they themselves must destroy and then preserve. Side by side in the large room that smelled of candles, stone, dry wood, the sharp farm instruments that for some reason had been removed, they considered the problem. Stubbs said that they must look on the lifeless horse as a statue and nothing more—Mary Spencer understood what he meant— and that they had only to lift it upright and then hold it in place. Of course they would use the block and tackle, the chain, the lengths of iron. Mary Spencer, hands inside her shawls, asked how. Stubbs replied that if the horse was to stand, it must have a platform on which its hooves could rest. But since it could not stand of its own accord, said Mary Spencer, how was the full weight of the horse to be suspended? Would they fit the carcass with girths as if for saddles? Stubbs paused. He said the horse brought to mind the stable but that they must think not of what was appropriate to the living horse but the dead one. Butcher, said Mary Spencer, and surprised them both. Hooks, said Stubbs.

Using the forge and anvil and short lengths of the iron rods, Stubbs hammered out eight hooks modeled on the ordinary needle with the points curved upward and the eyes wide enough when cool to accept the long bar of iron that was half the weight of Stubbs himself. The hooks slid along the bar wherever Stubbs wished to place them, in the center of the bar was a ringlet large enough to hold a ship's prow to one of the docks in Liverpool. A corresponding ringlet in the ceiling beam, block and tackle between the two, the hooks driven into place between the ribs and under the spine of the subject, as Stubbs called the poor animal—and he and Mary Spencer could hoist to whatever height they wished the heaviest horse that could possibly be brought to their farm in Harkstow.

Stubbs sent out his request for horses.

The first appeared on a Sunday. A young boy bareback on a pony shaggy beneath its winter coat—long hair covered its eyes and most of its face—led an old gray horse into the barnyard on a length of rope. Stubbs and Mary Spencer stepped out and greeted the boy, Mary Spencer tried to talk with him while Stubbs inspected the horse, or Nan, as she was called according to the boy, who pronounced the name with a scowl to Mary Spencer. Nan proved to be a broodmare close to thirty years in age, Stubbs decided. She was healthy though thin, which was to be expected, and obviously was of no further use to the farmer who had sent her off with the boy. The boy said that the farmer offered the pony as well—the boy could return on foot if need be—but Stubbs said that Nan, who was hanging her head and looking at Mary Spencer with large blue eyes, was sufficient and that he had no use for a pony. Stubbs unfastened the rope, the boy hung it loosely coiled around his neck. Stubbs paid the boy for Nan, the boy said he must have the halter. Stubbs removed it, the boy rehooked the halter to the rope and let it hang at his hip. The gray horse was motionless and so was the boy. A breeze that was tinted the color of the sun on the horizon—a greenish red—and cold enough to make Nan shiver passed out of the barnyard, disappeared. At last Stubbs said that he had been brought up a tanner and that his mother was still proprietress of the family tanning business in Hull. Upon hearing what he had been waiting for, an explanation, the boy nodded, smiled, raised a finger as to the brim of a hat—he was wearing none—and prodding the pony with the heels of his boots that had once been worn by his grandfather—they were that large—he turned the little animal about and started back the way he had come. A short way down the frozen road he looked once over his shoulder, gave a short hoot of laughter, and sent the pony into a rolling, jouncing canter. Nan, still rooted where she stood, swung her long gray head, stared after the departing pair, and began to tremble.

The old horse waited stock-still while they lit the candles, donned their leather aprons, uncoiled the ropes. The interior of the outbuilding was no warmer than the exterior, yet Nan ceased her trembling once inside. She waited without halter or chain to hold her as they readied themselves to tie her feet, fasten the girths that would bear her weight—ropes and pulleys fastened from smaller ringlets in the beams above the girths—in the process of toppling her over and stretching her out flat on her side. Mary Spencer stroked the cool flanks, the serpentine head, but the old horse did not peer down at her, did not so much as blink or allow her breath to be seen in the watery nostrils or detected in any movements of the ribs that were silvery to both touch and sight. Why, the old horse was complying with her own fate!

Stubbs commented on Mary Spencer's revery and without her help tied Nan's front legs together, then the hind legs as well. He fastened the girths, drew the ropes taut, said that now he could not proceed unless Mary Spencer assisted him. She must hold the ropes, he said, while he leaned against the old horse and pushed her over, the blocks and tackle, regulated by Mary Spencer, easing the horse over gently and down. But here, surely, Mary Spencer thought, there would be a struggle, though nothing on Stubbs's face revealed the concern he might have felt.

But no, Stubbs pushed and Mary Spencer pulled, leaning herself backwards against the ropes—how easy it was to hold the entire weight of a horse if given the cleverness and resultant apparatus of a man like Stubbs—and the ancient mare obliged them without a shiver, allowed herself to tilt, go over and slowly down, even holding her head and long neck in the same plane as the body. Then she was lying flat on the stone, a statue indeed!

Stubbs had maneuvered the animal so that its neck lay across the trough he had cut into the stone of the floor, beneath the wall to the ground outside, where, though the earth was frozen, he had dug a pit to receive the twenty gallons or more of the blood that he would now drain from the veins of the placid creature. He knelt, scalpel and square of canvas in hand. Mary Spencer knelt at the head, assuming that for the moment she could be of no help to the dissector. Stubbs covered the head and neck with the canvas, told Mary Spencer that he would lift his side of it only and do his work swiftly, protecting her against the sight. They would see no blood since beneath the heavy canvas it would leave the body and return to earth with the creature's life, slowly, until the heart in its last contractions had pumped the animal all but dry.

Stubbs raised the canvas. From several miles away came the commotion of Lord Nelthorpe's hunt running to earth its fox. But before he could make the swift, deep slice he had envisioned, Stubbs withdrew his hand in astonishment. In a quick reflex beyond his control he pulled back from the horse. She moved! Nan might as well not have been tied, might as well not have had half her head covered like some prisoner facing execution. She raised her head from the floor, tossed it about as best she could, flung off the canvas, struggled with all the recovered strength she had once possessed, and did her best to kick, flaying her pairs of legs in a scissorslike motion, there on the cold stones looked as if she were flying in some sort of barbaric gallop despite the ropes. She thrashed her tail, heaved her ribs for breath, rolled her eyes, and, worst of all, cried out in tones that suggested human strangulation. She sweated, her coat glowed. In all her ancient being Nan rebelled.

Mary Spencer gave a cry. Stubbs a grunt. What now?

Then Mary Spencer again dared to approach the tossing head on her knees, cried the old mare's name in womanly compassion—Nan! Nan!—and cradled the wet muzzle, chin, cheeks in her arms. The rebellion ceased. The terror and fierceness left the eyes, the quieted blue eyes looked up into Mary Spencer's face, the woman rested the great head on her knees. The motion ceased, the body sagged, legs and tail again lay inert on the stone. The horse was stilled. In a quick whisper Mary Spencer told Stubbs to open the jugular vein as he said he would. Quickly!

When he was done, Stubbs said that Mary Spencer had been through the worst and could now bear as well as himself the various stages of dissection that were to come— from insertion of the iron hooks to disemboweling to the delicate work he would do on more than one horse's head. Whether as witness or assistant, he said, for her there would be no commotion as disturbing as the one they had just experienced.

That same day and the next Stubbs injected the major veins and arteries with tallow, and then on the third day he drove in the hooks and hoisted the old mare into full standing position, hooves on the plank, about eighteen inches from the floor. Now Mary Spencer understood that Stubbs had meant the word "statue" literally as well as figuratively and shared Stubbs's opinion that the dead horse—they had agreed to use her name no longer—looked exactly as she had in life but also that the gray mare standing in the candlelight of their outbuilding was more than similar to some historic horse statue in a village square. Mary Spencer was fond, as she said, of the animal they had managed to suspend in place—fond at least until Stubbs began the slow process of dissection. By the end of seven weeks, when the subject was too decomposed to be of any further use to them, Mary Spencer felt not fondness for it but revulsion, though still she helped Stubbs in the disposal and did not call attention to her emotions. She could not say which was the more oppressive to her, the animal's panic, scrutiny of a lateral view of a horse with only a portion of its skin and subcutaneous fat removed, fear of disease, or the signs of carnage in which they spent their days. But the more their work continued through the third horse, the fourth, the more she marveled at her Stubbs, who drew exactly what he had dissected and whose only emotion in their outbuilding was the pleasure of concentration.

Lord Nelthorpe wanted Stubbs to paint husband and wife seated side by side on their horses and facing the viewer. Lord Nelthorpe said that he wished the portrait to show himself and his wife and the heads and faces of their horses as in a mirror. Stubbs waited. Then he asked if His Lordship wanted the painting to include only partial busts of himself and wife at best? Lord Nelthorpe colored at the word, his wife smiled, Stubbs looked at them both and considered. Then he asked Lord Nelthorpe if it might not be to greater advantage if he painted His Lordship and Lady Nelthorpe from the side. The lateral view, he said, especially if Lord Nelthorpe's horse were positioned directly behind his wife's, would show much more of His Lordship, the entirety of his wife's gown, the full beauty of their horses, and as well would pay tribute to Lady Nelthorpe by allowing her to ride ahead of her husband. Lord Nelthorpe knew a great deal about horses but nothing about women or argumentation. After a moment's pause, his thick face settling into obvious distaste for the painter and pique at not having his own way, he agreed.

The first sitting was conducted on a cold day between two icy showers. The husband and wife rode out in front of Colwick Hall, and a groom positioned them as indicated by Stubbs according to plan, the husband's horse directly behind the wife's. Both horses had docked tails, the husband's horse was darker than the other and marked by two white stockings on the rear legs. Stubbs asked that the husband's horse be moved still closer to the wife's so that the gelding's head hung just above the stumpy tail of the mare. Lord Nelthorpe wore a long chocolate-colored coat, white britches, black boots half of the upper portion of which was tan. On his head was a small dark hat with a narrow brim, a thick braid of hair reached to his shoulders. He sat straight though somewhat round-shouldered on his horse and stared resolutely at his wife. But the wife, of her own accord and without a word from Stubbs, was looking unashamedly at the painter. And it was she who dominated the preliminary sketches and the final portrait.

It was no more possible for Stubbs to tell Lady Nelthorpe how to arrange her skirt than it was to arrange it himself. But no sooner were the horses standing front to back, parallel to Colwick Hall behind them—Stubbs had already decided that the handsome elongated manor house would stretch its pinkish brick from one edge of the painting to the other—than Lady Nelthorpe understood exactly what Stubbs wanted: a total view of her. Carefully she arranged the skirt of her riding dress—she was seated sidesaddle on her gentle hack—so that it flowed as far forward and down as possible from her upraised knee and as smoothly as possible down from that exaggerated curve she made of her body from her shoulders to the rear of the saddle. This portion of the skirt fell below the horse's belly, swept up again at a pleasing angle to where her right foot was concealed in the folds of cloth mere inches behind the silhouette of her horse's chest. Most important of all, Lady Nelthorpe's riding costume, or the one she had chosen for this portrait, was scarlet. It was a bright yet subtle scarlet that could not be ignored. The jacket and bodice and skirt covered her body completely, so that only the face and the briefest glimpse of a wrist were exposed, the skirt composing a triumphant scarlet triangle in a single sweep—in this way Lady Nelthorpe filled the portrait, though she was given no more space than her husband. Then, too, however, she wore a swollen black hat that topped her little head more like a mass of raven than ostrich feathers—which they were—and exaggerated for anyone who cared to see, as did Stubbs, the ordinary, unimaginative hat of the husband.

To the final portrait Stubbs added two dogs, a brown dachshund all but impossible to see between the front legs of the husband's horse, and a white foxhound bitch trotting head-high just forward of Lady Nelthorpe's horse. There had been not a day of sun when Stubbs made his sketches and worked on the painting—the canvas came to be mounted on two easels in the same parlor where he had painted the son—but Stubbs gave it a clear sky and a gentle mass of clouds that corresponded inversely to Lady Nelthorpe's shape on her horse. He had the pleasure of painting the husband's horse without its ears, a detail that went unnoticed by Lord Nelthorpe. Lastly Stubbs heightened one small additional point of red, Sophia's lips, and this small point of color matched to Stubbs's thorough satisfaction the entire scarlet riding costume of Lord Nelthorpe's wife.

On the day that Stubbs completed the portrait, when beyond their parlor the world was enclosed in the season's hardest shell of ice, Stubbs found himself speaking as he had not intended. He said that the time would come when Lord Nelthorpe would have his wife painted out of this portrait. Not by himself, Stubbs said, but by some other artist. Just as she had vanished under his hand from the painting of her son, so the husband would rid this second painting of her presence.

With better cause, she said, and laughed.

But he will destroy the painting then, said Stubbs.

Confidence, confidence, she answered. At least they two would know for the rest of their lives that she was there, in both portraits, just as he had painted her.

Invisible, said Stubbs.

Invisible or not, she answered.

There was a crash, a shattering of ice, the breaking of frozen briar and bramble. Mary Spencer gave a cry, Stubbs dropped his instrument, made for the door. Mary Spencer reminded him of the apron. He removed it.

As soon as he stepped from the outbuilding, Stubbs confronted at a short distance Lord Nelthorpe, master of Colwick Hall, his clothing wet, his stirrups iced, his complexion both red and white, his pink coat pulled askew with vigorous action. His hunter was tossing and throwing his head, rearing, its broad chest wet and slick. And horse and rider were motionless in fury at the edge of the copse that bordered the outbuilding. Lord Nelthorpe yanked on his horse's mouth, leaned to the side to keep Stubbs in his line of sight.

"Not one of mine, Stubbs!" he shouted, and pointed with the handle of his crop toward the windowless outbuilding. "Not one of mine!" Then, applying his spurs and pulling hard on the reins, the horse squealing and chopping the undergrowth, Lord Nelthorpe wheeled him about and was gone.

What I think analogous to the serratus minor anticus arises from the sternum and part of the first rib or collarbone and from the cartilaginous bindings of the second, third, and fourth rib near their joints to the sternum. It is inserted into the shoulder blade and tendinous surfaces of the supraspinatus scapula. . . .

Blood vessels of the neck and abdomen exposed. Many of the muscles of the upper hind limbs removed. . . .

Shoulder joint and ribs exposed. Only the deepest muscles are left. . . .

Few muscles and some ligaments remain. The nervous supply to the fore limbs stands out clearly. . . .

The sciatic nerve can be seen in the upper hind left limb. . . .

quadratus

abductor brevis

abductor longus

origin of the rectus

caudal view of the skeleton seen obliquely from the left

7

"MR. STUBBS, help me!" cried Billy Cobb, Lord Preston's smallest stableboy and the only boy in the entire Preston stud who could soothe the unpredictable violence of Whistlejacket.

"Mr. Stubbs!" cried Billy.

Whistlejacket was Lord Preston's favorite horse, his once personal hunter, winner of a considerable purse at Malton, a larger purse at Hambleton, twice winner of the King's Plate at Lichfield. When Whistlejacket's portrait was done by Stubbs—upon the recommendation of Lady Nelthorpe to her friend Lord Preston—the great horse's hunting and racing days had long given way to his life as the most notorious and valuable horse in Lord Preston's stud, and the most dangerous.

"Oh, Mr. Stubbs!" cried Billy.

Whistlejacket was the tallest and largest-boned horse ever to be used for racing in Lord Preston's time. The animal stood more than seventeen hands at the shoulders or nearly six feet. The circumference of the narrowest part of his leg, measured below the knee, was ten inches, while the narrowest circumference of his hind leg, similarly measured, was nearly eleven. His color was as rare as his size and viciousness. He was a palomino, shocking to find among the blacks and grays, browns and chestnuts ordinarily raced or hunted. The fetlock of the right hind leg was white. Otherwise he was a mass of darkened gold set off by the silky white of the mane and tail and the bright black of the hooves.

"Oh, Mr. Stubbs, save me!"

Billy Cobb was in his twelfth year but as short and frail as a child. He had a round face, black, frightened eyes, a perpetual well-intended smile, frizzled hair. He wore a black hat inside the stable and out, torn knee britches, a shabby little coat in Lord Preston's colors—yellow with red piping— to mark his proud station as a stableboy. His effect on Whistlejacket was like that of the pony or kitten beloved by a stallion and used to calm him. Billy could walk between the legs of Whistlejacket in total safety, just as the favored tabby kitten may arch its back and rub itself against the hooves of its stallion without fear of being crushed.

"Mr. Stubbs."

They set to work in early summer, George Stubbs and the little stableboy and the stallion whose reputation only made him the more appealing to the painter. It was simultaneously warm and cool, the scent of yellow hay and the smells of horses reached them from the stables. The first time Stubbs saw Whistlejacket in daylight outside the stall he knew the horse's measurements without taking them and thanks to his sixteen months of labor on lesser beasts was as familiar as no one else could have been with all that composed the bulk of this prized animal. And Whistlejacket showed no signs of having aged, standing head high in the sun, though he had nearly reached the age of the oldest horse that Stubbs had anatomized and drawn on the farm in Harkstow.

Stubbs painted only in the two or three hours that followed dawn while Billy Cobb posed Whistlejacket close to the painter—the portrait was to show the horse life-sized and filling the canvas, which was nearly nine feet square— or walked the heavy stallion up and down until Stubbs needed to see his subject standing motionless again and no more than a body's length from the canvas. A long rope descended from the halter to the miniature fist that held the end, often Billy Cobb was lost in the horse's shadow. Billy's voice was as small and piping as a bird's and during those morning hours, walking or standing, he sang to the horse in tones Stubbs was pleased to hear. Man and horse and boy were alone, there beside the end of the long and partially empty wing of the stable where the famous stud was sequestered from the aggravations large and small that sent him into panics or rages. To their right a field rolled away to the horizon. From a distant stall came the struck note of the tine of a pitchfork.

Whistlejacket could not be posed as Stubbs was in fact painting him. The horse was to be rearing up in profile, its thick hindquarters borne above the bent hind legs, the front legs dangling as for some menacing purpose, the head, which was nearly malformed in its closeness to the skull that shaped it, turned partway toward the viewer as if the viewer himself were the cause of the horse's fear and rage. The ears would be flattened back, the nostrils of the smallish nose distended, the eyes filled with abhorrence. There would be no rider, no saddle or bridle, yet the effect he wanted, Stubbs knew at once, was of a horse who has just startled and thrown his rider, the horse in his helplessness about to crash down and with his front hooves crush the rider sprawled beneath him. Stubbs saw it all, knew exactly how to show the horse at his most violent even while it was esssential that Billy Cobb keep Whistlejacket calm, at peace, so that without distraction Stubbs could select whatever detail he wished to paint. Only a tranquil scene, Stubbs thought, would allow for the creation of the majestic terror to be shared by horse and viewer alike.

"Mr. Stubbs! Mr. Stubbs! Help me!"

It would have been natural for Stubbs to portray Whistlejacket at rest, the better to conceal his defects of character, and a lesser artist might have done so. But Stubbs could not. He was driven to make the grandeur of Whistlejacket's derangement—for such it was—explicit. For five weeks Stubbs thought of nothing else, though he told Mary Spencer about the unexpected vision that would burst at last on Lord Preston and though, less frequently, he imagined Lady Nelthorpe driving her carriage—light as a feather—behind a rounded pony from Colwick Hall to Lord Preston's estate for her first sight of Whistlejacket attacking his invisible victim. Stubbs liked the contrast, infrequently as it came to him, and knew that Lady Nelthorpe herself would value the fantasy.

The nose appeared on the white canvas, the neck, the hooves, the croup, the tail. Each late morning Stubbs covered and carried his work and easels into an empty stall for safekeeping, each dawn retrieved them, mounted the canvas in the light he could smell. Three legs, the belly, the completed head too small and serpentine, curiously feminine for the size of the aggressive animal appearing here and there on the white field. The chest that might have worn the harness of an Egyptian chariot. The last leg, which was the second hind leg, clothed in its white stocking. Stubbs asked Billy Cobb to lead Whistlejacket closer, to stand, to pull down the head. The ears flicked forward, Stubbs smiled. The forehead was unmarked. Stubbs returned to the pictured horse and added a small jagged blast of white between the eyes.

Was it done?

Stubbs heard the last cock crow and held his brush poised, looked from the painted animal to the gently receding boy and horse, the head lowered and giving Billy Cobb an affectionate nudge that sent the stableboy almost off his feet. The pair turned, started back toward Stubbs, who knew all at once that he must now see his painting in a different perspective. Awkwardly he lifted the canvas from the easels and leaned it against the rough-colored brick wall of the stable. Twenty paces away he stopped and turned.

"Mr. Stubbs!" cried Billy Cobb all at once. "Help me! Save me!"

And there they were, horse and boy before the painting, Whistlejacket, docile only moments before, now for the one and only time staring at himself as in a mirror and already rearing, rising like his counterpart in a murderous mood. He tossed his head up, to the side, Billy Cobb hung high, feet off the ground, swinging in circles like a rabbit in the jaws of a terrier.

Stubbs ran toward the pair. Whistlejacket went down and up again, attempting to slash the image of himself with his front hooves.

"Save me, Mr. Stubbs!" cried Billy Cobb, swinging and twirling helplessly on his rope, but it was the portrait Stubbs meant to save. Whistlejacket's ears were flat to his skull, he rose, twisted, screamed, again struck out at the painting but merely tore the air. Another moment and the thrashing horse would destroy not himself but the irreplaceable work of art. Stubbs ran between horse and painting, risked the hooves, flailed his arms, shouted, tried to seize the rope but could not. He saw his maulstick—it was too slender, slight—then luckily a length of wood the proper size for his hands and long and heavy enough to deter the horse. He snatched it up and, bracing his arms, waited until Whistlejacket dropped again to all fours, and brought the stick down between Whistlejacket's eyes.

"Off!" he shouted. "Away!" And he managed another blow to the horse's head.

Whistlejacket swerved away from the painting, settled to earth, immediately grew calm. Billy Cobb regained his feet, steadied himself against the trembling chest, tottered, and stood upright.

"You'll be hurt yet," said Stubbs, laughing and collecting his breath. "Take that horse from my sight. I am finished."

For background Stubbs added only a pea-green primer, convinced that anything else—trees, gorse, stone fence, sunlight—would detract from the portrait, and determined to allow Lord Preston no say in the matter. When Lord Preston first viewed Whistlejacket, he studied the work for a considerable time and then smiled, complimented Stubbs sincerely, and said the painter had seen what no one else— including the horse's owner—had seen, namely, that the living Whistlejacket was a bronze statue. Think of it, he said, a bronze statue!

* * *

Thus closed the career of this celebrated artist, in profession unequaled, in old age kind, in private life exemplary. By the number and quality of his works he raised a monument to himself that will vie with time. Valuable Man. Oh, Valuable Man. . . .

III
THE
FOX HUNTER

8

IN THE FIRST week Alexandra and I went through the photographs that she had already collected. She had kept them in leather albums, photographs of the two of them together and then all the rest. She was missing from most of them. But she showed me Harold's infancy, his youth, Harold as a well-known horseman. Newspaper clippings, featured pictures in event catalogues, professional prints. When they married, Alex was a mere girl, as she said, though she was in her early twenties. Harold was a decade older. And Alex had begun to save every photograph in which he appeared as soon as she met him, which was several years before their marriage. I had never seen her collection—now removed from the albums, sorted, assembled in manila filing folders—and I said that I never would have expected her to show such an interest in Harold as others saw him. All that time. All that devotion. She did not answer. Then I said that anyway she had already composed Harold's photographic biography and that there was no need for me. But she said that Harold had never seen her albums. No matter, I said. The work was done. She shook her head. More than once, she said, he had told her he wanted Mike to do a study in photographs of the life of the old Master of Foxhounds after his death. And she had never asked him what he meant? She had not. However, she said, I could photograph anything I wanted from her collection.

"You mean I'm to look at all this, decide what I like best, and photograph it over again?"

"Yes," she said.

"Alex," I said, "it's pointless. And it's boring."

"I'll know the photographs are yours, just as he wanted. When you're done, it won't have anything to do with all this."

"When I'm done, what happens then?"

"To all my girlish collection?"

I nodded.

"Out it goes," she said, and smiled.

I selected little from Alexandra's filing folders. Within days, within nights, safe behind my sitting room door, aware of the silence Alex must have imposed on Steepleton for the sake of my work as she called it—her work in fact—I discarded, figuratively, decades of her naive industry. I went as quickly as I could. Privy to her secret—no one else had seen Alexandra's albums—I enjoyed the judgments that I began to make as swiftly as the decisions I make while taking photographs. So much concealed pride in her husband. And lack of taste? Yes, the woman I thought I knew for her aesthetic mind and quiet spirit, easy enough to see whenever she played Haydn or put her arm around Virgie, revealed poor taste in every scrap she had saved of Hal. Years of the emptiest sentimentality, nights of unjustified self-pleasure.

Yet alone in the dark of my darkroom, in the depths of Steepleton and locked within the nights of my daylight hours, this image and that began to tell their story.

The photograph for which the artist strives has no story. Story is the anathema of the true photographer. Narrative, dull narrative, of interest only to those who sit or stand at the frame's center or lurk at its edges trying to squeeze themselves into the picture, is what the chronicler of the family hopes to preserve. The most significant snapshot—

that of the family in mordant stillness or pretended action—is nothing but an object to jog memory and ease the present or, worse, to instill memory in children, which cannot be done.

However, if Alex was sentimental in the very act of collecting images of her husband, and sentimental—indiscriminate—in the images she chose to collect, still there were those I could not toss away—figuratively. I looked at them, rephotographed them, enlarged them, looked at them wet and dry, unable to stop myself, because these partially revealed narratives were not run-of-the-mill. To me.

I could not bear Hal's infancy—bonnets, long dresses, English carriages—and not much of his adolescence or young manhood. But what about the full-page photograph of Hal at the sophomore dance? Or the Hunt Club champagne get-together? Or Hal sharing first and second prize with B. Coyle at a local Pony Club event? Hal posing a group of swimmers in a photograph captioned "A Tangle of Limbs"?

The sophomore dance appears ordinary enough. Dim but spotty light, the glare of a three-piece orchestra, milling young men driven only to hold and touch their stupefied companions in long dresses. It is a dark black-and-white picture with crowd and light holding in place Harold Van Fleet, the tallest adolescent of them all and the only dancer, at momentary rest, who is confident of the manhood he has already achieved.

My first enlargement shows that his partner, wearing her short-sleeved ballroom gown, is heavier than she ought to be. I know the color of the hair that hangs on her thick shoulders and obscures her flattish face as well as I know the color of her dress. Blond. A blond girl in her first ballroom gown. Blue. Harold prefers green or all the shades of red from pink to blood red and he dislikes taffeta, which is what his partner is wearing. A blue taffeta gown. Her large bosom is larger still for its gardenia. There are perhaps a hundred gardenias hastily affixed to the gowns of the girls in that room, yet Harold sees only his partner's, is aware that his own chest has not flattened that gardenia in the expected fashion.

Harold does not show his disappointment, if he in fact finds his partner disappointing. Instead it is the girl who is disappointed, who is as crushed as her gardenia is fresh. She has suffered some confusing blow to her expectations and sense of self. Until now she has considered herself of good build and worthy of kisses—she is fifteen years old—and after six years in dancing school, where determination overcame the lassitude of chubbiness, she knows that she is a passably good dancer.

The problem is that Hal has danced only the first dance with her, nothing more. Not even the last, though in the yearbook photograph they stand together. And why? Because of the girl in the obviously green dress who appears just behind the seventeen-year-old Harold Van Fleet. She has dark hair, short and bobbed, and is looking away from both Hal and the camera. But she is smiling. She's as old as Hal, she's been perspiring, she is receptive but not immodest. She is touching his hip in my third enlargement while he is groping for her hand and staring without awkwardness or shame at the camera. He has danced all evening with the girl in green. Her stockinged legs are as slim and tight as a woman's.

The xylophone ripples into its last note, the cymbal shimmers to stillness, the music is smothered in the noise of the crowd.

Late the next morning Walter T. Van Fleet receives a telephone call from the girl's father, who complains of how Hal has treated his daughter. Walter frowns. Walter and Hal discuss the problem, Hal calls back the father, apologizes, agrees that his invited partner of the night before did not deserve humiliation. Is there an explanation? There is not. Any excuse? None. Only the father, the injured girl, the inexplicable hurtfulness that is the heart of humiliation and the cost of maturing. Did Hal understand what he had done? Feel the brief heat of responsibility? He did. Years later he could summon into his face with ease that first unwanted but instructive warmth. At times it appeared unsummoned. But he was not cruel.

Harold's sophomore yearbook photograph was the brief narrative of youthful choices—aesthetic, moral, personal—

and was one view of Harold's early decisiveness. But for Alex it was only a picture of Hal at a dance.

"A Tangle of Limbs" slipped by, buried again in the folder I had too hastily opened, closed, and returned to the stack without seeing the caption or paying attention. But bathers? A composition of bathing girls in the life of Hal? Quickly I retrieved the folder, went back through it twice—no girls in white rubber caps—and then slowly, impatiently, until I held before me a snapshot—that's all it was—so unusual, despite its ordinary contents, that it had to have been taken by someone whose eye, those years ago, had been as good as mine was now.

Who was he? Why no credit with the caption? Why didn't I recognize the style of that composing eye? Dead, I knew at once, and he couldn't have left behind many photographs like "A Tangle of Limbs."

Wit and mystery despite banality.

Giant boulders that form a solid sheltering wall, still water rippling as with light on oil, the old white hull of a sailboat bisecting the photograph from left to right, and sprawling on the deck of the weathered hull, the girls. Five slender ropes rise to the right of the center toward an invisible boom, two thicker ropes slope carelessly from the stern of the hull into the water, sagging, bearing no weight, serving no purpose. It is all clear, black and white, sensible at first glance. But how many girls are on the hull of the boat?

No answer. The girls are uncountable.

The snapshot is cropped so that above the hull and girls and across the width of the picture only as little as possible of the rocks is shown. There is twice as much water below the girls and hull as expanse of rocks above them. The water looks as if it had been painted rather than snapped by a young artist—my age, I know at once—using a box camera. All is arranged so as to concentrate on the sprawling girls. Yet those girls, symbols of summer, cannot be counted.

For the viewer's first few appreciative minutes their number is not a question, does not come to mind, exactly as the other incongruities hide themselves in the first delight of seeing that magic snapshot. Number of girls in the picture? Why, five of course. Four girls lie with their legs hanging over the edge of the hull, behind them sits another reading a book. Five. Well, yes, there is one more pair of legs close together—crossed at the ankles in fact—and dangling down toward the water precisely in the middle of the snapshot. The legs of the dominant four present to the viewer listless near verticals that catch the light and the viewer's eye as well, the pair of legs crossed at the ankles is hidden behind the thighs and calves of the middle two, hardly more than repose and modesty in dark shadow.

But wait. A portion of a head shows behind and resting on the shoulder of the girl who usurps the center of the picture. A portion of a leg rises out of the left-hand edge of the picture, there is a knee floating upwards to the right, another white sphere, again on the left, reveals itself as the cranium of a head in a white skull-tight bathing cap. And actually another head is resting on the turned-up hip of the girl reading a book. So the number has now changed to nine. Then there is an upraised arm half white, half black, thanks to light and shadow, whose hand, no doubt gripping one of the ropes, disappears off the top of the picture, as severely cropped as the wall of rocks. The fact is that the total number of girls is indeterminate, yet there they are, sprawled in the heat and candor of the summer.

To be fixated on this snapshot, aroused in the best of erotic humors, is to be fixated on the swimmers' legs. The now five major actresses in this still life—so far it is a still life—are by no means hanging both legs over the edge of the low hull with its flaking white paint and chipped dark paint of the deck, insofar as the deck is not smothered beneath the soft and deliberately vulnerable bodies of the girls, who, except for the blonde absorbed in her book, appear to be sleeping. Not at all. Five are lying so that only one leg of each hangs down, three from the knee and two from mid-thigh. The girl to the extreme left has the knee of her other leg, the left, sharply raised and bent but nonetheless touching the tilted head of the star—the girl in the middle is obviously the star of this cast—while the girl on the right, whose head is invisible, has her right knee sharply raised and tilted outward from herself and the hull toward the viewer. The girl in the center—the young star—dangles both legs over the edge of the boat but somewhat apart, the right toward the water, the left across the knee of the second girl from the right. But it is the girl on the far left, she who lies with her head tilted so far back that only the white triangular underside of the jaw is visible, who sprawls in unmistakable invitation, legs wide and crotch of the old white tank suit purposefully exposed. She defines the rest of these uncountable beauties, who in their mass are lying against each other in spent anticipation.

Not a drop of water glistens on their suits or arms or legs: their exhaustion does not come from swimming. But they might have raced, laughing and splashing each other, and have merely lain long enough in the sun to dry? Then why didn't they remove their caps? And why the black gloves worn on the right hands of the star and the suggestive girl to the viewer's left?

Where did Alex find this snapshot? Why did she save it? Who clicked the shutter of the box camera? Where is Hal? Where is the narrative?

Then, having searched for half an hour, I saw the telltale detail—how could I have missed it?—and the puzzle disappeared, the still life became narrative. On the chest of each girl's white suit was the initial *P*, clearly visible on the plump chest of the girl I had dubbed the star, and that *P*, distorted out of definition on the chests of the other girls, stood for *Psi*, the twenty-third letter of the Greek alphabet. Sorority. There it was. How like Hal to have fought off his brothers until he had arranged the girls and gotten his picture.

A one-night outing, a day and night at the lake. Earlier that day at the local store Hal had bought his box camera and for a single purpose—to entice the girls to submit to his whim and, ulterior motive, to begin a singling out of the one girl among them all whom he had selected for the empty but still-warm deck of the hull that very night. Not the star but the girl to the far left. The girl with the cocked knee and white crotch who was his favorite, just as she was mine.

"Done!" cries Hal, and I look down again at his snapshot—he did not bother to complete the roll, left the camera behind on a table in a rustic cabin, eventually lost track of the snapshot—and the girls leap to their feet, tear off their caps, dash to the bow of the hull and around to the jetty, where Hal stands in his white shoes, white shirt, white ducks, and like childish maenads—they are young girls still in school—they gather and clamor about Handsome Hal, aged nineteen, until with one mind and eager bodies, they push him off.

Long before dusk those girls know which of them will go down to the boat with Hal.

"A Tangle of Limbs" was a snapshot that was taken when Hal was not yet twenty. Slowly I turned it over and found what I knew I'd find. Initials. H.O.V.F. Nothing more but enough. I still have that snapshot. Alex never knew it was gone. To her it was only the endearing silliness of Hal's senior year.

The Pony Club photograph is an example of quick and easy journalism. Flat. But it has its interest. B. Coyle is flanked by two men, her fiancé and winner of third place, the caption says, and H. O. Van Fleet, second prize winner. B. Coyle holds the cup. All three are smiling, B. Coyle's fiancé goes unnamed, and even in the grainy photograph his smile is strained, though he cannot know that he will bear no name when on the following day he sees himself beside B. Coyle. Furthermore, he has won many a third prize so cannot be unduly disappointed. And jealous of his prospective wife's blue ribbon and silver cup? Unlikely.

The three figures stand in a row, B. Coyle herself over-come with surprise and excitement, unable to believe her good fortune, and H.O. Van Fleet, easy and oddly content with his second place. Yet at that time Harold, who was about my present age, was the most accomplished horseman of our region. How could he have come in second to B. Coyle's win?

Three horses attempt to poke their large heads into the picture, but though each bears a ribbon affixed to its bridle, clearly in this picture the horses have been forgotten.

The fiancé is holding B. Coyle's upper arm with his left hand, B. Coyle's wet face, wide eyes and helpless smile indicate excessive exhilaration, Hal's face shows that he is pleased even as he looks off casually to the left, away from the other two. The fiancé ordinarily holds B. Coyle's arm in public, at social occasions or out walking. He is proud of her. And ordinarily B. Coyle tolerates with ease her fiancé's possessive hand. But now? Now the spectators are milling about, horses are being unsaddled, the engaged couple and H. O. Van Fleet are posing before the camera. And B. Coyle is standing closer to Hal than to the man whose anxious grip is his pleasure and privilege. So close to the apparently indifferent Hal that the fiancé, who feels but fails to understand what has happened or why there is such space between himself and Barbara, yet considers it unseemly to close that space at the moment of being photographed, merely waits with his left arm awkwardly extended. His brow glistens, his lips are wide, pinched, and parted, his left arm, so often his proud signal of approaching new status—the marriage will occur in three weeks—strains away from his side unnaturally, more straight than bent.

Since protocol required that B. Coyle be positioned in the middle of the three winners, Hal, who is tallest, destroys the symmetry of the picture. Dominates it. Throws it off.

This Pony Club event has resolved into a contest between male and female, man and debutante. H. O. Van Fleet on At-a-girl, B. Coyle riding Silker, and the unusual gift of difference not only in age but gender—men are the most likely finalists in this group of riders—heightens both the silence and applause of the spectators, puts them happily on edge though the end of the day is as hot as it was at noon.

The turf inside the open arena is torn, the rails are back in place on the highest jumps, Jim Stiller, who is always counted on for a good fall, has been safely taken off in someone's station wagon to Emergency. The fiancé, valiant to the last, is guaranteed third place if B. Coyle holds her luck in this final test.

H. O. Van Fleet, after glancing once at his opponent, who returns his glance and smile more expressively, goes first. At-a-girl, a hefty mare, starts off. The crowd gasps. Faster and higher go this favorite rider and the mare more hot-blooded than any stallion, their timing closer to the flow of blood and rate of hearts than to a stopwatch. Halfway around and H. O. Van Fleet will win. Off to the side Silker fidgets—he is next and last—while astride him B. Coyle watches. But is she watching the performance, the horse and rider together, or the rider?

Then down they go, H. O. Van Fleet and At-a-girl. Their only fault—a bad one—of the event. After a perfect score and nearly record speed, this fall. The crowd groans. B. Coyle is not smiling. The fiancé is standing beside her, hand on a stirrup, sometimes slipping his hand up to the ankle of her black boot, and he is pleased at this turn of things and, while still looking at the fallen pair, says a few words to B. Coyle. She does not hear.

At-a-girl is on her side, legs jerking. Hal has performed his usual trick of not falling or allowing himself to be pinned beneath the animal's side, instead propping himself with reins in hand, one foot on the ground and the other leg across the horse's back. No one in the crowd likes to see a horse and rider go down, yet with Hal and At-a-girl things are different. She is known as a scrambler, as a horse who, slipping onto her side in a curve, nonetheless scrambles up again, rider in place, with mere seconds lost. It is the same with Hal. He has learned his trick and never falls free of At-a-girl but keeps his balance, maintains his control, stands at precisely the right moment, foot on the ground, calf across the saddle—like a motorcyclist when his machine has slipped from beneath him in a fast turn taken at too steep an angle—so that when At-a-girl is up and away, he is there, with her, swiftly and securely mounted as if nothing had happened. No lying half stunned while the horse clumsily regains its footing and goes off at a hopeless canter, stirrups tossing. No lying together in an embarrassing heap.

But now, in this of all accidents, Hal is slow while At-a-girl exerts herself as usual, rises. Hal is in place but gives a little bounce in the saddle—no one sees it—and gathers At-a-girl too slowly. Too cleverly to be detected. Intentional. It is Hal's only dishonest act as a horseman and he completes the course, applauded, more than ever admired and satisfied with his skill and confident that B. Coyle is oblivious to what he has done to help her.

Off she goes, large girl trimly gotten up in boots, britches tight in the seat, black coat—buttoned—velvet-covered hunting cap with its cork lining and little brim in front, and her face is flushed, her eyes bright. She is breathing hard already but from some personal excitement of her own, not exertion. The exertion is to come. Silker feels her rhythm in their first slow canter—she is holding him in—and the sensation of her thighs and calves against him. Her heel grazes his belly. He snorts, tosses his head, she leans forward, pats him on the neck with one of her gloved hands, whispers into his ear. He listens, waits for the surging that the girl on his back will soon demand not with whispers but with her crop and the pressure of her legs.

First obstacle. The second. The first turn. Faster. The crowd is forward, waiting. If she makes one fault, H. O. Van Fleet will win. Yet it would be amusing, pleasing, if B. Coyle could go into her wedding having beaten H. O. Van Fleet and won this particular trophy and blue ribbon.

Silker and B. Coyle take the brush fence nicely—where has that girl gotten her inspiration?—and coming out of it, B. Coyle allows herself a glance into the crowd and not, as everyone thinks, at her fiancé, who is at the rail, but at H. O. Van Fleet, who has avoided the fiancé and stands between two admiring men who give him plenty of room. His returning glance, he knows, is all the girl needs.

Halfway through the course. And she has no time or concentration to spare for looking into crowds, especially since she knows that he has borrowed a pair of small binoculars. As they land after going over the simulated brick wall, she feels herself flop once in the saddle—not good—and lets Silker feel the crop. By the time they start into the in and out, all is well and Silker proves not even close to knicking one of those white bars.

Three-quarters of the way around. Horse and rider are exuberant. Then they approach the second brush fence, higher than the first and treacherous, concealing as it does the shallow pond they must clear from a blind start. She remembers—here Jim Stiller exercised his usual poor judgment and got a dousing as well as his broken arm. But B. Coyle applies the crop—there are those who can hear its thwack—and she and the little Thoroughbred, his color lost beneath the darkness of his sweat, land well beyond the edge of the water.

Then worst of all, up the wooden steps of the artificial hill and down the steep slope that throws Silker's croup high behind him, and on to the jump of two sets of bars placed about a foot apart—they take it well—and into the highest jump of the course. B. Coyle thinks there's no stopping her—only Hal can see that she is holding her breath as Silker's rear legs leave the ground—and suddenly feels herself at the peak of the ascent, of the world, and needlessly glances back at Silker's rear legs tucked up perfectly, with six inches to spare.

They land amidst clapping, she loses her black cap, now, at this last moment, and shakes free her hair. She gives a rueful smile, throws back her shoulders, and rides forward to H. O. Van Fleet, who will kiss her before the fiancé has a chance to move. The black cap rolls to a stop.

So the engaged couple and H. O. Van Fleet pose before the camera. The narrative, like the black cap, stops.

Who was B. Coyle? Buse, of course. Our own Buse. That's how long ago she and Hal first met, only weeks before the weddings that were imminent for each. No wonder Buse was such a friend of the family.

And here, finally, was a Hal it had never occurred to me might exist. A man like the rest of us. Had Alexandra really known him? I thought not.

9

ALEX HAD NOT yet done anything with Marcabru, the heavy, dark bay stallion ridden only by Hal, who always said that the horse was gentle enough for a child. Hal had bought him against everyone's advice, especially Alexandra's. Marcabru had a long history of shying, rushing, biting, kicking, bucking, rearing. A dangerous devil, said the man who sold him to Hal, who only laughed and scoffed at what everyone knew. No other horse and no other man—other than Hal— was safe around him, though he tolerated Harry. Harry took no nonsense, Hal said. It was simply a matter of hitting the bay's nose with the flat of your hand—hard—the moment the ears went back or the teeth showed. Hal bragged that he himself had not once struck Marcabru in all the years he had loved the horse, showing him, hunting him, putting him to stud. And Marcabru had not once misbehaved for Hal. But the horse was Harold's one indulgence, according to Alex. How, she asked, could Hal claim, as he did, that Marcabru looked like Whistlejacket? Bay, she said, was as distinct from palomino as boy from girl—a figure of speech that surprised us all. Yet Hal insisted that Marcabru was descended from Whistlejacket, despite Alexandra, who said there could be no such line of descent at all. But Hal always objected to her

117

literal-mindedness. How, he asked, could she allow mere color to blind her to what he saw so easily? Marcabru was as tall as Whistlejacket, as heavy, and the heads of the two horses, unmistakable in shape—long, thin, and narrow, bony, all eyes and nostrils and teeth—might have come from the same mold. Why, he said, she had only to see the horse at sunset to understand.

Was he serious? No one, least of all Alexandra, knew.

I tried to tell Alex that there was a certain truth in what Hal said, but she only laughed and refused to listen. The horse that was kept in the most elaborate box stall in the stable duplicated in every way the horse forever rearing in the grand salon—except for color, which, as Hal said, meant nothing. Even their dispositions were the same, I said, given the little we knew about the historical palomino. To which Alex always answered that Harold had better watch himself around that horse, no matter how long the brute had been at Steepleton without causing trouble.

From the day Marcabru arrived, exploding with kicks like gunshots inside the van before it had even stopped in the cobbled stableyard, Alexandra's dislike of the horse had been as uncharacteristic as Harold's excessive love of him. Marcabru was seventeen hands tall, heavy, with bones so large that they might have belonged to an animal of some ancient mightier species. He bore not a trace of white and except for the hooves and tail and mane—all black—only his eyes and nostrils and mouth could be distinguished in color from the great mass of rusted midnight brown. Marcabru was Harold's joy and perhaps his joke.

And finally Harold had died because of Marcabru. Not riding him, not in a high fatal accident while jumping, as he would have wished, but on foot, alone, trampled under the hooves of his favorite horse as the light began to fade in the stall.

How had Alex managed to tell us? I never understood how she brought herself to that account. But she had.

Softly, the day before the funeral, when Buse kept herself from crying and Virgie showed no grief except pallor, Alexandra told us what had happened. Marcabru, she said, was still quivering when Harry had found them.

Why had she not gotten rid of Hal's horse, the mistake of his life?

"He's still here?" I asked.

She nodded.

"Why?"

"I won't sell him or give him away," she said. "Naturally. And I can't have him put down."

I waited.

"I just can't," she said. "Not yet."

"It's the best thing," I said.

She looked away.

"Then sell him," I said. "For stud. He'd be safe enough on a stud farm."

"I'll wait. I have to wait."

The stable was L-shaped, made of ivy-covered fieldstone and roofed in slate. A high, handsome archway connected the two arms of the L and served as entrance to the stable and also led into the courtyard that was formed on two sides by the building and on the others by high walls and chestnut trees. The driveway leading down from the house to the stable was cobbled, as was the courtyard. I had always liked nothing better than to approach the stable on a frosty dawn in time to see someone leading a horse from one wing of the stable to the other, to see the man—or woman or girl—and then the horse, neck sloping, head nodding, the colors of his blanket obscured in the new light, hooves making the long-familiar slow sounds on the cobblestones, the elongated moving animal framed for a moment in the arch. Then the diminishing sounds of horse and person disappearing into the seclusion peculiar to stables.

But the place was silent, inactive. Midway down the driveway I could hear only my own footsteps, my breathing, nothing else, even when the stable came into full view. There was not a voice to be heard from within the depths and opulence of the two ivied wings, not one horse passing across the archway, not a sound. But I knew that Marcabru was in there, peaceful enough at the far end of the long arm of the L, which faced the house so that I could see its entirety. The windows, one for each box stall, were larger than such windows usually are, and clean, reflecting the dawn light. Each was contained and protected in a dormer. Set like a large gem in the ivy.

I stopped, took the first photographs, concentrated on the invisible stall at my far right. A waste of opulence was what I saw, the beauty of the place ruined by what had happened. It would come out in my exaggeration of the frost on the fieldstones and slate above. It was dawn in a season that felt more like early spring than late fall. Harry, I thought. Harry is in his office. Waiting.

He spoke my name behind the half-open door of the office that adjoined the tack room. I paused, said, "Harry," and entered. Nothing in this room suggested hunting, point-to-point racing, show jumping, dressage. Not a poster, photograph, mare and foal on a calendar. No brass paperweight in the shape of a horseshoe. In Harry's office there was not the faintest smell—of hay, manure, leather, oil—that helped make the rest of the stable the comfortable place it was.

"You want to take his picture," Harry said, moving from behind his desk to sit on the edge of a table.

"Alex called?"

He picked up a pencil—a Japanese drafting pencil—and looked at me.

"I'll lead him out if you like," he said.

I told him that first I would go alone and photograph him as he was. In his stall. Harry glanced up at me. I said that after I took the first photographs, I wanted to take more—in the stableyard, perhaps in the ring, several on the driveway up to the house. Saying nothing, he conveyed his disapproval—he had work to do, the horse was difficult. Harry was not quite as I remembered him—the gray hair, lips more obviously bitten, eyeglasses out of character with the ruthless horseman. But he wore the same kind of English shirt and tie, tweed jacket, the same trim jeans and jodhpur boots.

"So you were telling her what to do with the horse," he said.

"You had a long phone conversation," I said.

"Breakfast," he said.

Harry's apartment was above the office and included a

large modern kitchen. I had seen Harry's apartment once when Hal took me up unannounced. His dining room chairs were Italian, the sofa French. I thought of Alex eating bacon and eggs at 4:00 A.M. with her stable manager. I remembered an oval daguerreotype on one of the walls. His father.

He put down his pencil, glanced over my shoulder to the half-open door. "You didn't tell her the obvious," he said.

"Oh?"

"There's only one thing to do with that horse. I've been arguing with her, but she won't make up her mind."

"What do you want her to do?" I didn't like his "she" and "her."

"The horse is too dangerous to sell, too good to put down. No one would want him for stud—not with his history. Especially now that he's killed a man."

"Is there anything else?"

"Marcabru," said Harry, still glancing over my shoulder, "would make a fine gelding. After, I'd discipline him for a month or so. Then anyone she wanted could hunt him, show him. No better jumper in the world."

"Alex should have him gelded then," I said.

"Of course."

"But obviously she just doesn't want him around," I said. "Doesn't want to be reminded."

"She'll get over it."

"I'll let you know when I'm ready," I said, starting out.

"We've moved the horses nearest him to the other wing," he called after me. "But don't startle him. Don't open the stall. No flashbulbs."

"My flash," I said without looking back, "is infrared. Invisible."

The corridor was wide, not a cobweb hung from the rafters. Harold had made a special trip to France to find the design he wanted, and at the last minute had found the perfect model in the stable of a friend's château. There were white enamel name plaques on the box stall doors, the stalls themselves were made of hardwood planking. Sometimes an extra window of stained glass cast decorative blues and yellows into this sequestered place. Yellow lamps hung overhead from brass chains. Halfway to Marcabru's stall, other horses heard me, thrust out their heads, watched, pulled away. Gambit. Pete. Goneaway. Ministerial. Nimrod. Waffles. Alex's horse, or favorite of three, and Virgie's and mine—Lady Di, Misty Rose, Martha, in that order—were in the other L of the stable along with the rest of the mares that had been moved as far as possible from Marcabru. Harry was taking no chances. I stopped to stroke a few noses, say their names. Gambit, Pete, Goneaway. Big geldings, all of them. I walked on, stalls to my right and left were empty, doors hooked open, hayracks still filled with hay.

The box stall at the end. Larger. Lighted by two high dormer windows instead of one. And the mahogany—the stall was built of solid mahogany—was stained a dark brown and polished. The name plaque was twice the size of the rest and edged in scroll. His blanket—brushed wool of red- and cream-colored checks—was folded over the partition.

Marcabru was in there. I whistled softly, waited, looked over the top of his door. He was standing backwards, croup in my direction, head down. The black tail hung to the straw that was fresh, a nearly transparent yellow as hard and glossy as the shed bodies of insects. He knew I was watching but kept his back to me. Remote. Harold died of a failed heart only minutes after they dragged him from under the hooves of this horse and out of the stall. A failed heart, kicked to death, what did it matter? Somehow I had expected evidence of what had happened, but there was none. Only Marcabru the same as ever, Hal gone.

As soon as I began to photograph him, he moved. One long step and he was at the hayrack—iron rods, the skeletal shape of half a rounded basket—and stretching, pulling down mouthfuls of hay. Right lateral view, horse caught in the slanting light behind him. I clicked the shutter faster than I could count, with each exposure stopping the impatient head as it yanked down the hay.

"Marcabru," I said. "Come here."

He froze, long wisps hanging out of his mouth, ears suddenly flat to his skull. The tail flicked.

"Come on," I said, "over here."

I was silent and he went back to his munching. The head yawed, he chewed with the hay sticking out of the sides of his mouth, the jaws worked in an exaggerated sideways motion. He didn't mind the clicking camera, but my voice put him immediately on guard. The ears relaxed, one of the sharp black hooves gave a thump.

I put the camera in my pocket, stood close to the door, watched him. Then, without looking down, I reached for the bolt, and as mindless as the horse, stealthy—I had begun to think of him as stealthy—I pulled back the bolt. Smooth. Not a sound. I asked myself what I was doing. I had never paid much attention to Marcabru in the past—why now? If I needed help, there would be none. I shrugged, pulled the door just wide enough to enter sideways, did so, drew the door shut after me. It was not bolted, which the horse couldn't know but I did. Escape. Easy escape.

Nothing happened. If I had expected to see for myself how swiftly Marcabru's mood could change, I was disappointed. But I had no expectations. No fear. I thought of Hal's name—Harold—then began clicking the camera. I moved to the rear of the horse, to his other side, drawing closer to him with every step. And the longer I stayed with him, the larger he became. He was taller at the shoulder than my six feet. I could not see over the top of him. I lowered the camera, held my breath, reached up and cupped my free hand on the top of his shoulders, rested my hand up there. He pulled at the hay. The light was coming down on us, I stood ankle-deep in the straw. His color was a shiny cross between the brown of petrified wood and the black of coal.

As quickly as possible I began photographing the entire interior of the stall, careful always to include some detail of the horse in each exposure. I half crouched, pointing the camera across his chest and up toward the opposite wall.

"What are you doing?"

Harry.

"What are you doing?"

His voice was soft but unpleasant in a way I'd never heard before. The stall door was open just enough to allow him to stand there facing Marcabru and me, coiled lead dangling from his right hand. I straightened up as best I could, brushing my trousers.

"You can see what I'm doing," I said.

"Yes," he said. "Asking for trouble."

"It's safe enough," I answered. "As you can see. He's in a good mood."

"After what I told you," Harry said. "I warned you to leave him alone. Look where you are. Even a child knows better."

He was right. I looked around quickly and saw that I had gotten myself into one of the far corners and that again the horse had swung his croup in my direction. It was a first rule—when in a box stall with a horse, stay in front of his head. If the rule is not obeyed, the horse is free to do what he likes, from shoving you against the wall to worse. It's a way to get hurt. The youngest child—the novice—learns to follow this rule without thinking.

"All right," Harry said. "Come out of there."

He allowed me past.

"Well," he asked, "have you had enough?"

"No," I answered. "I'll take some more, as I told you. In the stableyard."

"He'll smell the mares," Harry called over his shoulder, but I walked on ahead of him, quickly, wetting my lips and paying no attention to Pete, Gambit, the rest of them. I could not complain, could not tell Alex what had happened, could not get back at Harry.

There was a figure silhouetted in the archway. Virgie. As I drew closer, I was both pleased and irritated at the sight of her. From the waist down she was dressed like Harry in jeans and jodhpur boots. But her jeans were loose, baggy, and the Norwegian sweater she had bundled herself into was sizes too large, a mass of white yarn turning yellow. She took pleasure in hiding herself, as now, and in exposing herself—hers was the hard body of a child—which she did when wearing her boots, her elasticized white britches, her little black coat that nipped in at her waist.

She stood in the hollow archway with each forearm stuffed into the sweater sleeve of the other, two forearms for each sleeve.

"Early," she said.

"Early for you," I said.

"Fight with Harry? You look gray."

"You're grayish yourself."

"Mother says you're taking pictures."

"Just an impulse."

"Pictures of Daddy's horse, Mother says. How can you do it?"

"It's what she wants."

"Poor Daddy. I'm for putting that horse down. But I'm a minority of one."

"No, you're not. But anyway, I'm just taking a few photographs of Marcabru. Not many."

"You can take some of me."

I smiled.

"Virgie," called Harry, his ugly voice reaching us over the slow, clear rhythm of Marcabru's hooves on the corridor floor. "Virgie! Misty's waiting for you."

"Meanwhile," she whispered, "back at the oasis the Arabs were eating their dates."

"What's that supposed to mean?"

"He hates jokes, that's all. I get sick of him."

"You better do what he wants," I said.

For answer she turned and in her Norwegian straitjacket, which was how I thought of it, she strode off into the stableyard. I found her sitting on a stone mounting block on the far side. Cold, I thought. Cold stone.

Marcabru stopped short as soon as Harry led him from under the arch.

"I thought I'd taught you something," Harry called. "Obedience. Discipline."

"I'm just watching," she called back. Her head was propped on her hidden fists, her toes were pointed together. Her eyes blinked, her large teeth still looked strapped and wired, though an indifferent young dentist had removed the braces years before.

"Harry," I called, "bring him over here. The light's perfect."

Marcabru backed halfway into the arch, Harry coaxed him out, again the horse balked. Carefully Harry drew down the head, said something. And the demons fled, the panic dissolved in the eyes, the body gave in, man and horse walked forward, stood where I wanted them. Harry spoke to Marcabru. Virgie laughed. I had caught Marcabru in his loping walk—each stride covered about four feet—but now I was circling him, camera clicking. He was standing tall, head high, and seemed to be listening to something, a distant sound that only he could hear. Or was he pricking up his ears—those pinched, telltale ears—for Hal? Or for the hunts that had already filled, would fill again, the silence and the emptiness of this stableyard? He could not have been larger, more handsome. Except for the peculiar head. But Marcabru dangerous? Malevolent? He certainly didn't look the part. Again I thought that Hal had been right all along. I noted that Harry was keeping his back to the camera.

Suddenly, before we could stop her, Virgie rose, crossed the cobblestones, ducked under the slack lead rein, and stood peering up at Marcabru's head. That's all it took.

The horse reared. Harry called out Virgie's name, Marcabru reared again, pulling Harry off-balance, crashed down, and kicked. Virgie did not flinch or move.

"Let me have him!" she said over her shoulder. "I can hold him!"

"Get away!" cried Harry. "What's the matter with you?"

"Do as I say, Harry!"

"Look out!" he yelled.

Circling to the left, then right, lunging forward at Harry, then dropping his haunches and jerking backwards while I circled the three of them, clicking the camera, and Virgie, hands on hips, still refused to move yet remained untouched. Some kind of beast might have been clinging to Marcabru's back, so helplessly did the big bay submit to his fury. He appeared not to see Virgie, as close as she was, but only to smell her scent. And it was Virgie's scent that Marcabru was trying to escape. I knew the first photographs I had taken would prove the best—those of Marcabru alone and half rearing with noble balance.

"Alex is going to hear about this," Harry said, just as he leapt, caught hold of the halter, yanked down the head, and began slapping the tender nose. Then, before the horse knew what was happening, Harry led him with no more trouble out of the stableyard and back to the waiting stall.

Virgie, who had hardly moved, was out of breath, quivering. She dragged the voluminous sweater over her head and followed Harry. At the archway she paused and looked back over her shoulder. "That horse," she called, "hates women!" Then she was gone and from the depths of the stable came the faint sound of whinnying.

10

I'M NOT IMPETUOUS. I'm not impulsive. I'm not impatient. I live by design and the mildest kind of calculation, allowing for circumstance. But by the same rule I do not procrastinate, especially when it comes to seeing the first prints of pictures I've just taken. Here I submit to the press of eagerness, a need to discover as soon as possible what I've done. It's only what the developed film shows me that I care about.

But after devoting two rolls of film—not many—to Marcabru, I waited. It was not a deliberate hesitation, I was hardly aware that I was violating one of my few habits. Perhaps I left those two rolls of film—seventy-two exposures—in the darkness of their canisters—two polyurethane canisters small enough to hold as a pair in the palm of the hand despite the enormity of their contents—because for once I was putting off a pleasure. Perhaps I thought that the developed film would prove me as good a photographer of horses as I was of women. Or perhaps I had no motive for waiting, only some vague premonition that told me to put it off.

At any rate I left the two canisters undated and unidentified on a shelf above the long stainless steel sink in the darkroom and, without thinking, went to Harold's rooms.

Lights of various kinds, including a Chimera, which is a light diffuser on a boom and wheeled stand like the ones used for carrying infusion sacks in hospitals, along with tripods, extension cords, cameras, all this I moved from the whiteness of the studio adjoining the darkroom up to the foyer, up the wide stairs, down the corridor to Harold's door. It was closed. Not a sound in Steepleton. All three women, I thought, must be down with Harry, which I knew wasn't true.

I hesitated, understandably. I did not know who had last been in Harold's rooms. Alex? Or had his private rooms been vacant since his death? I could not remember when I myself had last been invited into Harold's study, where occasionally we sat together in leather chairs and talked about horses. I knew only that nothing had been touched in that apartment—Alex had told me in passing—yet as I opened the door I wasn't even convinced I would see the space and furnishings as I'd seen them for years.

I went in, forgetting about the equipment. I went in alone, closed the door, stood still a moment, then slowly moved from cold room to room, trying to persuade myself that Hal would have approved of my presence. The long table, the age and use evident in the heavy chairs—animal claws cupped their brass wheels—the dark blue drapes tied back from the windows, the smell of tobacco hanging there forever. And best of all, Hal's prize work of art, a large wooden articulated model of a horse standing on a smaller table with one front leg raised. It was a painter's model and not a work of art. But to Hal it was art.

I stopped at the table and with a finger pushed the raised leg down. I remembered that horse in simulated trot and canter, rearing up. It could move exactly like a living horse. Even its lower jaw worked. I waited, lifted up the front leg as I had found it, and moved on.

I hardly paused in the bedroom but rather stood in the doorway and surveyed the room that had been left as I had seen it only a few times in my life. The four-poster bed, larger than most antiques of its kind, was unmade, the bedclothes were tossed back, flung off, and the closet door was open to all its hanging clothes and darkness. And here was the raised window. Alex was right, no one had been here since his death, as if the chill and dust and ashtrays weren't enough to tell me that I was the first to enter. Unjustified though the thought might have been, still it seemed to me that Alex and Buse, who long ago had decided to dispense with a maid and do the housework together, should not have left this room as Hal had left it.

I closed the window.

I avoided the bathroom for the time being.

Soon, with the Chimera in place in the study and ready to flood that room with an inescapable flat bright light, and with the other pieces grouped where needed, thick electric cords tangled across the floors of Hal's privacy, I turned the apartment into mere rooms where I stopped short or strolled like some sort of director on a dead set.

Later I discovered that I had spent as much time photographing the wooden horse as, long ago, I had given to Sylvie in her sharkskin shorts. The light was intense, subdued, intense. I shifted the tripod, changed the film, aimed the camera into all the angles the horse demanded, worked so as to allow it to stand in its familiar context or so that it would exclude everything else in the first print that would emerge in the darkroom. I raised his right front leg to join the left and balanced the horse backwards as in dressage, then caused him to rear up or to stand, head lifted, stock-still, a gift for the most finicky of horse painters.

I rolled up my sleeves, turned to the desk. And there, suddenly, I saw Hal's sculpted meerschaum pipe. It had belonged to Walter first, then Hal, the drawn breaths of father and son were still inside that pipe, I thought, as I took it from the open silk-lined case and propped it against the blue and white china tobacco jar. Made in Holland. Decorated with horses, riders, hounds gathered to hunt. And a quarter filled with the dark blend the men had smoked until Walter died and Hal changed to a commercial brand. The bowl of the pipe nearly filled my palm, it was a burnt orange in color, its stem was amber. But climbing up the bowl, not quite to the top, were two fighting stallions, rear hooves braced on the shank of the pipe. Their manes flowed, their front hooves pawed the bowl and struck at each other, one horse was already besting his fellow. I photographed them. Their final portraits—two—would have nothing to do with remembrance, unlike the pipe itself. One sight of the pipe and I smelled its rising smoke, saw the smoker. The camera, at least mine, did not admit the past. No matter what Alex expected, my photographs, especially those I took that week in Hal's room, would stand only for themselves.

Morning. The rest of the afternoon.

Now and then Alex interrupted, insisted I ride with her down trails concealed beneath winter growth or down the hard roads that must have had destinations though I could not remember them. Nothing moved, there was no sound. Except for our horses and, overhead, crows too cold to alight. Alex complained about me in her bantering voice. She was worried. I was not a very nice companion. Next time that she wanted a riding partner, she said, she would choose Harry.

Later I made Hal's bed, cleaned up the bathroom, laid out his clothes. Tie, shirt, everything. I decided on a pepper-and-salt tightly woven suit that was the lightest in his wardrobe, and so changed the season. And a narrow blue silk knitted tie—he owned no ties that were not knitted—and dark blue socks. I folded a white linen handkerchief, put it in the breast pocket of the suitcoat. I spent a morning arranging all this on the foot of the bed and then changed the entire array to hunting clothes, the tall narrow boots with their tan tops standing toward the edge of the bedroom rug, a large silent oval whose borders fell into no recognizable design and which contained nothing as identifiable as, say, a lily. I spent a day and night on a portrait of the boots.

Once when it was raining, I untied the drapes, turned down the bed, switched on the light in the bathroom, and left the door ajar, for no reason other than to photograph the bed without—unmistakably without—its sleeper.

In the bathroom I concentrated mainly on the tobacco-colored stains that could no more be removed from the marble—the sink, the bottom of the tub—than could the veins that were inherent to that cold limestone as smooth as soap. It was while photographing the folds in the shower curtain—Hal never took showers—that I allowed my shadow to slip into the picture. It was a rare error. I shook my head, knowing at once that I would destroy that particular negative, no matter my certainty that in the finished photograph the shadow would no longer have been there.

His fountain pen, a hand towel. A pair of socks bearing his initials, a worn place in the rug. His wallet left on the desk, the famous tiepin, which consisted of a long needle topped by an oval smaller than a woman's smallest fingernail and containing a wolfhound's portrait on a blue background—I made no distinctions, could find no hierarchy of values among his furniture, his clothes, his effects. So I had no choice and could only exhaust the possibilities of what was there, giving importance to the large and small, the personal and impersonal alike. In the end nothing was impersonal.

I forgot what I had photographed, what I had not. Would I ever be done? On I went, changing focus and filters, giving what must have been an hour to this, another to that. I found no letters, no correspondence of any kind in Hal's suite. Yet I made no effort to find letters. I was not prying.

Significant, insignificant, all of it.

As I had restored the bathroom as best I could to its original condition, so I tried to repair the damage wrecked by my ideas as I went along in the bedroom, the study. But I could not. Nothing was where I had found it. I had disturbed it all. Ruthless determination, I reminded myself, and continued.

All this time, amidst the sound of light, which for me was louder than the shutter's clicking, there was something that refused to shift into view but remained always on the edge of what I saw. Often I worked by repetition, for the third time moving equipment into the study, then the bedroom, the bathroom, disturbing the latest order I had tried to restore to this part of a room, to that, starting over. Disrupting everything. Hadn't I done it all? I had. But repetition is the most effective method.

It was while tying back one of the drapes, whose twin was properly looping like a miniature stage curtain, that over my shoulder I recognized what I had not seen, had wanted to see, had actually seen all along—the connecting door. I let the drapery fall—one tied back, one hanging, since imbalance is pleasing only when intended—and faced the door that gave Hal access to Alexandra's rooms and she to his. At that moment I could think of nothing but the concept of access and its corollary, lack of access. A door that was central to the privacy of two people was unlike other doors, including those of bedrooms, for instance, which are usually left open. I wiped my forehead on my rolled shirtsleeve, thought of the times that this door, only a few steps from me, had been opened, closed. When? Only at night? Had there been designated hours? Signals?

The connecting door in Hal's suite looked the same as the those leading to the bathroom, closet, bedroom, outside corridor. It was the same size, of the same dark mahogany panels, set into the same kind of frame as the others. But it must be different, I thought, and forgetting photography and my reason for being in Hal's suite in the first place, I stepped to the connecting door and saw, first of all, that the door was made secure not by a conventional lock and key but by a harmless enough appearing dead bolt. Or strictly speaking, it was the small brass oval knob of the dead bolt that looked harmless. I turned the knob, felt the bolt sliding free, and saw—my second surprise—that the connecting door opened into darkness about as deep as my shoulders were wide, and faced a door that was exactly its duplicate. Sound, I thought. When both doors were closed, no sound could pass from one set of rooms to the other. And when they were locked, neither one partner nor the other could pay the sort of swift and intimate visit inherent in the very definition of connecting doors. Furthermore, I now discovered that there were oval brass knobs controlling two more dead bolts on the insides of the doors. Each partner was in control of the other's access. Or lack of it. Each partner's privacy extended to more than soundlessness, if desired.

I had been able to open Hal's connecting door, which meant that Alex had not wanted or needed total seclusion when she had last safeguarded her sleep or merely her time alone beyond the darkness and dead air between herself and her husband. But then I discovered that she had had no choice in the matter. The second connecting door was bolted from the inside, from Hal's side of Alex's door, that is.

If, without hesitation, I had opened the door that I thought connected the two apartments, shouldn't I have known not to so much as touch the second? Hal's door was one thing, Alex's another, especially from where I stood in the airless semidarkness between them. Of course I knew enough to step back, to make Hal's door secure again, though the reason for such security was gone, and return to my work. But not me. Not Mike. It was a small temptation in fact, yet irresistible. So with as much stealth as possible I reached out two fingers, seized the knob, turned it. Then the doorknob. And standing so close that I might have pressed an ear to the wood to listen, which did not occur to me, I extended my arm and felt as much as saw the door moving inward. It was about a third open. I had not taken a step into the room I could now partially see.

A portion of wall that was papered in a fading parchment color bearing still fainter decorations of blue fleur-de-lis. A table, a white vase, pink roses. Carpeting. And the bed, not in full view, still larger than Hal's and covered with a quilted satin spread the gray and yellow tints of old bone. Alex was lying on the bed on her stomach. Her face was turned away from me.

I stood there—uninvited—looking at Alex. And the best to be said was that I made no noise. Of course I had not expected anyone in her apartment and certainly not Alex herself. Unthinkable. But there I was in her open doorway for no reason. Lack of decorum can be unpleasant. Lack of reason culpable. And I had no excuse, no reason. But at least she had not taken off her checked shirt, her jeans. Only her boots, and her stockinged feet—black silk stockings with jeans and jodhpurs, I thought, and smiled—were not anything I shouldn't see. But then she spoke, without moving, face turned away from me.

"You can come in if you like," she said.

So she had known all along that I was there and yet had not rolled over to greet me, or risen to an elbow, or laughed, had not done or said anything I might have expected and that might have spared me the embarrassment I rarely felt.

Alex was an active woman and never one to retreat to her rooms for a rest or nap. But there she was, prone on her bed, boots off, wide-awake and as good as asking me to come in. And suppose she had withdrawn to her bedroom for this hour—several hours—during the entire week or more that I had spent in Hal's rooms only two connecting doors away?

"Thanks," I said, but stepped back and drew the door closed as gently as I had opened it. Left it unbolted. Then I bolted Hal's door. Suddenly the room meant nothing, the lights might have belonged on another set. I could think of nothing but the darkroom and the two canisters that awaited me. Why did I feel such a need to develop those films? I did not know, do not know now. But at the sight of Alex and the sound of her voice I could do nothing, speak to no one, take no more pictures, do nothing until I had developed those two canisters of film.

I forgot to close the hall doorway behind me and went back. Midway down the sweep of the main staircase I heard Buse calling us to lunch. I continued around to the door newly made out of a closet door beneath the staircase and down the steps on the other side—no more closet—to the fresh whiteness of Steepleton's renovated cellar. Fluorescent lights, soundproofing against distractions, the whiteness of pure sterility.

The darkroom at last. Door locked behind me. No intrusions.

Never was I more alert than in the total darkness required for the moments it took to unwind the two spools of film out of the canisters and onto the three-inch reels and then to fit each reel into its stainless steel cylinder. Working in the dark was my first pleasure. To reach for what you know is there, to feel it, to be aware of the speed of your fingers and the cool surfaces always familiar, to hear the sound of the film against film and then the slight plastic-on-metal sound as the black lids are twisted into place on the cylinders—when nothing exists except invisibility and the tactile sensations that accompany the first swift gestures in the habitual process of bringing pictures to light—this beginning of the process is the simplest of its pleasures. The most promising. I work alone. I think of nothing.

As the timer sounded, I was already turning on the lights, removing the film from the cylinders, cutting the film into strips like short lengths of kelp, hanging the wet strips of film to dry. I left the darkroom, looked for Buse and Alex and Virgie in the kitchen—no one was there—went up to my rooms, waited. Then I returned to the darkroom.

Printing, enlarging. Brass pipes that reminded me of the interior of a submarine, amber-colored safelights overhead. I went through motions. I tried not to look. Embryonic figures submerged in trays, features like minnows half under rocks or undulating under the surface of their rectangular pools— I refused to look, tried not to recognize this or that moment I had spent with Marcabru in the stable or cobbled yard. Why? Because something was wrong. First one print and then another told me what I did not want to believe. And I, generally fortunate enough not to feel strong emotions, knew the beginnings of anger.

In the finishing room I fed all seventy-two prints into the drum dryer, then into the print straightener. Riffling through the entire lot of enlarged prints that were now flat and dry, I thought that somebody had tampered with my films. Such tampering is an act of personal destruction. Hurtful. Despicable. Inflicting injury on the photographer through his work, not by destroying his films altogether but by marring them.

The finishing room, adjoining the darkroom, was as white as the rest of Steepleton's renovated underground space and was glazed by the same intensity of fluorescent lights overhead. I smelled the light, the heat in the room. I stood there with my disfigured prints in hand. Alone. Arbitrarily I pulled one from the sheaf and was hardly able to see the horse's neck and head. Because close to the center of that print was an X carved by a woman's fingernail.

Then prints in hand I moved.

Back up the freshly varnished stairs, back up the broad stairway, down the corridor, straight into Alex's suite, bypassing Hal's, and into her bedroom. I had no reason to believe that she would be there, but she was. Head and shoulders propped on pillows, a knee raised, a hand behind her head, last light at the windows and brightening the translucence of the white drapes. Expecting me?

"Mike," she said, "what's the matter?"

I could not blame Alex for what had happened, and yet breaking my angry silence by a gesture only, I threw the prints onto the bed beside her. A few fluttered to the floor.

"For God's sake," she said, "what is it?"

"Someone," I said, in a voice that was not mine, "has tampered with my films. Ruined them."

"Oh, Mike," she said, "are you sure?"

"Look for yourself."

Slowly, eyes on mine, she picked up one of the prints, glanced down, looked back at me. Nothing more.

"Well," I said, "don't you see it? Indelible marks, scratches. There's some sort of ugliness on each one of them. Probably done by a woman."

She glanced down once more, still said nothing, then held out the print, which I seized from her fingers. I looked again. Then I stepped to the window. Here was more than an X. Someone, with a nail file perhaps, since it needn't have been a fingernail, had attempted to scratch out the entire image. A disarray of slashes, a cruel cross-hatching, back and forth, up and down—the attacker had obscured as much as possible of that picture. Despicable? It was vicious. But then I began to see the fragments of photograph beneath the scratches and I stared, tilted the print, then took another from the scattered heap beside Alex. Another. All the same. Not my photographs.

"Alex," I said softly, too shocked for anger, "it's worse. I didn't take these pictures. They're not mine."

She tried to look at me with a comforting expression. "Of course you took them," she said. "There's no one else."

"You of all people think I've made a mistake? On the identity of my own work?"

She nodded. "I don't understand how your pictures got defaced," she said, "but they're yours. They have to be."

"I'm not wrong," I said, and sat on the edge of the bed, gathered the prints together, began to look. She reached her free hand behind her head, switched on the reading light. I moved closer, frowned, prepared to study the prints. Nonetheless in peripheral vision I saw that Alex was concentrating on me just as I was concentrating on the prints. The look on her face had nothing to do with the light tone of assurance she had just expressed. She was waiting.

Slowly I turned from the first print to the second, the third. More slowly. It no longer mattered that the prints were defaced. It no longer mattered that the pictures were not mine and that mine had probably been destroyed. Because these photographs were of Marcabru, true enough, but each one of them included human figures as well. And each was blurred.

"Marcabru," I said as if Alex wasn't there at all. "And Hal. There's Hal."

The light was dim, the pictures had been taken indoors, inside the stable, in front of Marcabru's box stall, and all were blurred, some more than others, because of what could only have been unnatural haste. The speed and furtiveness of desperation. Light touched the bolt on the stall door and the bolt was thrust home. Marcabru's head was ungainly, wrenched high. His teeth caught as much light as the brass bolt and his eyes were staring out with that terrible luminous look of the frightened child. Much lower was Hal's face—I was sure of it—and the man's expression was as violently distorted as the horse's. And the next and the next. Human figures—two—turning this way and that, blurred, in front of Marcabru. There was another horse.

"He wasn't alone," I said. "Why did you claim he was?" I expected no answer.

The pictures that were most blurred were clearest. I did not want to look, but I did. Who could have turned away from those pictures?

Noise. Kicking that would have smashed the planking in another stall. Hal trapped, two figures rushing about. Women? I thought they were. The saddle in a heap in front of the box stall, bridle only half removed from Marcabru, reins flung up, hardly distinguishable from the scratches. The second horse was docile.

"There's a second horse," I said.

"Lady Di," Alex said. "In heat."

Marcabru is charging, crashing, slipping, trying to turn.
No wonder. And Hal is trying to stop him though he knows
full well why his horse is crazed and that the animal cannot be controlled, even by Hal himself. Marcabru kicks,
squeezes Hal against a wall, attempts to batter his way
through the stall door. Here, in this picture, he has gotten
one leg hooked over the door. He's squealing. The women
have not had time to remove their hunting caps and the little
black caps dart this way and that, smaller than thumbprints,
smudged. The mare waits.

"The second woman," I said. "Buse?"

"Virgie," she said.

Mother and daughter. Wife and daughter.

Against my will I searched through the prints until I
found what I wanted. The stall door. Unbolted. No mare, the
stallion in a corner—not much of him to see—no human
figures. Hal facedown in the straw.

"Who took the pictures?" I said. "Buse? Harry?"

She did not answer.

"Do you know what you've done?"

But of course she knew and there was no need to answer.

"What now?"

"Nothing," she said. "Nobody knows what happened."

"Not even Buse?"

She shook her head.

"Harry?"

She shrugged.

"You. Virgie. Harry."

"And you," she said.

"And the photographer," I said, my tone of voice as serious
as hers.

She nodded.

"Hal was in a good humor," she said. "He led that horse
into the stall and got as far as taking off the saddle. The stall
door was closed. The last thing I ever heard him say—he
called out to me over his shoulder—was this: 'Too bad
women can't be more like horses!' He laughed, poor man.
Imagine that."

11

I HAD ALMOST totally recovered from my helplessness at Hal's funeral. Was I now to suffer the violence of the way he died? And condemn Alex? Condemn Virgie as well? Fall victim to a justice that in its simplest form is revulsion? I should have, I might have. But I did not. Rather, sitting on the edge of Alex's bed and from a handful of photographs beginning to understand what had happened, I felt instead fascination, incrimination, relief. I was already Alexandra's accomplice.

Did Hal deserve the fatal accident contrived by Alex? What had he done to drive his wife, a woman of irreproachable character, in courtroom language, to devise such an ingenious and reprehensible scheme?

I did not ask, but Alex herself wanted nothing more than to tell how deeply she had been injured. And Virgie too had been injured. By now it was evening and I was becoming used to her deceptions.

Buse set dinner places for herself and Virgie in the kitchen, without a question fixed trays so that Alex, claiming nausea, might try to eat something upstairs with myself as companion. On Sundays, when there had still been a maid at Steepleton, Alex and Hal had always eaten breakfast in Hal's study or her sitting room. One tray, Alex's, was white and sparsely decorated with small floating roses. The other, Hal's, was an oval of polished reddish brown rosewood whose folding sides and legs were held in place by small hinges of tarnished brass. It was Hal's tray that Buse now prepared for me. Steak for Buse and Virgie and me, tea and toast for Alex. Buse and Virgie didn't want wine—Buse was drinking scotch—so I put a full bottle on my tray.

"Mother ill?" asked Virgie.

"That's right," I said.

"She'll be fine by morning," said Buse.

"That she will," said Virgie.

Buse and I carried up the trays. Alex, wearing a French silk chiffon peignoir and sitting nearly upright in bed, did in fact look unwell. We settled the tray across her lap, I pulled a chair to the bedside and propped my tray on my knees. Buse closed the door. Then I brought a glass from the bathroom, half filled it from the opened bottle, half filled the wineglass, which I gave to Alex. We shared the steak by the light of the reading lamp just above her head.

The first she knew of Hal's infidelities, she said—I smiled at the word—was Buse. I asked if she was serious. She was. Did she mean that Hal and Buse had had an affair? Buse, she answered, had been Hal's mistress for as long as Alex had been his wife. Or almost. Not quite, since for about three years Alex had lived with Hal happily and proudly. Then Hal had declared that he wanted Buse for his mistress. Didn't he bother to keep the matter to himself? No, Alex said, the opposite. He wanted Buse to live at Steepleton, and simply declared his wishes. The whole thing was open. Had I not seen Buse every day of all the years I had been a member of the Van Fleet family? I frowned. And did I think that Buse was just a friend in the house? I nodded. Well, Alex said, Buse was closer to a second wife than a friend. The only thing in Hal's favor was that he had had the decency to keep her out of the house when his father was failing. And he had kept her away from the old man's funeral.

I said nothing.

Hal had bought a new car, a large brown sedan with an interior of tan leather, and in that car Hal was driving himself and Alex back to Steepleton after having been to a neighbor's—a large place, a horse farm—for dinner. It was an early night in midsummer; Hal was dressed formally, Alex was wearing a long dress—green—they were driving with the windows down. Hal complained of his back and sat at the wheel as formally as he was dressed. But he was cheerful, he drove slowly to please her, he had not drunk too much. Occasionally he rested his free hand on her knee. In the semidarkness she smiled. All was well. That night, she thought, their connecting doors would be open.

Then he pulled over and stopped. She did not ask why but wondered. At last Hal said he was going to buy a pony from their dinner host.

"A pony?" asked Alex, who was genuinely amused. "Why on earth a pony?"

"For our children, of course," said Hal.

"But we haven't any," Alex said with a happy laugh.

"We will," said Hal. "I'll just have the pony ready for the little fellow when he arrives."

"That," said Alex, "is the silliest idea you've ever had."

"I'm not given to silly ideas," said Hal. "Besides, it's a handsome pony."

And Alex was pleased to return his kiss there amidst the smells of hay and new leather and in the faint moons and half-moons of light from the dashboard.

They leaned back, Hal told her to open the glove compartment. She saw the package. For her, he said, and Alex, exclaiming and asking questions all the while, tore off the ribbon, the silverish paper, and opened the flat oblong box covered in black velvet. Pearls. A thick string of pearls.

"You've never given me a surprise present," she said, her voice sinking to a low pitch of love and submission.

"They go with your hair," Hal said. "Put them on."

She did so.

Then he said that Barbara Buse was coming to stay with them.

At first she neither knew nor cared what he had said, or thought she did not. The pearls were around her neck, she was feeling their oily weight with her fingers. Nonetheless she heard herself asking when.

"Soon," said Hal.

"How long will she stay with us?" asked Alex, still not interested in Barbara Buse.

"Indefinitely," said Hal.

Alex stopped moving her fingers, sat upright, looked at Hal, whose long face was as placid as it always was. He might have been talking about the pony.

"Indefinitely," repeated Alex. "And what about her husband?"

"Their marriage isn't exactly over," said Hal. "Besides, what can he do? He's no match for me and Barbara wants to live at Steepleton."

"Why?"

"Because I asked her to," said Hal.

"And me?"

"I told Barbara you wouldn't object. I assured her of that."

Suddenly Alex could say nothing more. But she could act. With both hands she tore the string of pearls from her neck and flung the pearls out of the car window into the darkness. She did not cry, she did not argue, did not shout at Hal. She felt that she had destroyed herself, not the pearls.

After a moment Hal leaned across her, reached into the glove compartment, and took out a long-handled flashlight as new as the car.

"Get out," he said. "Either you find every one of those pearls or you pack your bags."

Hal opened his door, switched on the flashlight, walked around to her side, and stood waiting. He did not open her door. Alex, who managed to understand that she could either tell Hal to take her home and lose him or do what he said and try to win him back, finally made her choice. At first she had difficulty opening the door, but did so. It swung out, Hal stepped aside, and Alex, stooped and defeated or perhaps sensible, she thought, gained her balance in the sweet-smelling night.

Fortunately, Alex told me, they were widening that portion of the road, an unpaved, untarred country road to begin with, so that the shoulders extended several feet before dropping into the drainage ditch and consisted of hard-packed sand and gravel. Otherwise, she said, she might have been crawling through high grass for the rest of the night looking for pearls. Hal aimed down the torch, its round beam was brighter than daylight and hurt her eyes. She saw the pearls scattered endlessly in the gravel. For a moment she wondered how to collect the tiny egg-shaped droplets, then gathered up her long skirt, making a safe pocket for the pearls, and awkwardly knelt down at the roadside and began her task.

"Alex," I said, interrupting her, "you should have left him. Just walked out."

"Mother always said that everything happens for the best. I think she was right."

"Everything?"

Alex smiled and went on.

When they reached Steepleton, Hal returned to his usual kindness. He opened the door on her side and helped her out. As they climbed the front steps, her skirt gathered at her waist, he guided her by the elbow. Alone in the cool darkness he steered her to his suite, locking the door behind them, and into his bedroom. No lights, but he needed none. He scooped the pearls into a bathroom glass, placed the glass on his bureau, then without a trace of roughness or anger he embraced Alex, flattening one long hand against the broad slope of her back where it descended into what Hal called her croup. His hand, she said, felt like a starfish.

Disheveled, stockings mutilated, knees skinned, joints aching as if she were an old arthritic woman when she was only twenty-four, and still tasting traces of humiliation, nonetheless she had never wanted Hal as she did now. She was shocked at herself. His fingers drew down the zipper that allowed her gown to fold open on each side of her bareness from below her shoulder blades to the cleft in her croup.

Hal was not in a rush. She groveled on his bed as she had at the roadside.

"Poor Alex," I said.

"Not at all," she said.

Buse was installed, Alex learned to put up with her. The pearls were restrung. At first the scales of Hal's desire were tipped in favor of Buse, naturally, the more so since her presence damped Alex's own newly found passion. Then the scales righted, Alex discovered that Hal enjoyed her as much as he did Buse, Hal's general pleasure in the situation, including his lack of discretion except at home, caused Alex and Buse to share a friendship that did not depend on Hal. And Alex and Buse both came to overlook those moments when out riding alone together with Hal, he referred to them as his two girls.

But the quality of life began to change. Hal grew bored with both wife and mistress and was disappointed with his daughters. He never recovered, or so he told Alex, from the death of his father. He began to drink. There were nights when he did not come home and Alex and Buse waited up together. There were times—not often—when he fell on the stairs. Then he began to bring home women.

"But, Alex," I said, interrupting again, "I never saw any strange women in the house."

"Harry put them up. But when it was late enough, Hal would escort them up to meet us. If we refused, he said, we would regret every moment of our lives that we had lived with him. As if we didn't regret those moments anyway."

"Alex," I said, "you still might have walked out."

"No," she said. "By now I knew it was impossible to reform him. But I was old-fashioned and Buse was naive. We loved him. At any rate, up from Harry's he'd come with his latest find. He insisted on introductions, calling Buse and me from our beds if necessary. Then he might take the young woman—she was always young—to his rooms or directly back down to Harry's. On those nights he made Harry sleep in the tack room."

"Alex," I said, "I've never heard anything so absurd."

"Absurd? Well, one of those young women was a waitress in a bar-restaurant. She was also an amateur parachute jumper. Think of it! She used to try to persuade Buse and me to take lessons. She said her boyfriend was an instructor. Boyfriend! At two A.M. and having to listen to that girl talking about her boyfriend and parachutes! She was serious. Small and lovely-looking with long blond hair and a complexion like cocoa and butter. I guess she was so athletic and had such a lovely color from being blown around on clear days in her harness. At least she could see that Hal wasn't fit for leaping from small planes.

"But I never knew what was coming next. I suppose another woman might have forgiven him or grown indifferent. Not me. I did not forgive him. Just as I never really forgave Buse, no matter how much we tried to help each other. And all the while I continued to love Hal."

"And Virgie?"

"Whatever he did to Buse and me, he did not want to hurt Virgie. He never felt affection for her, but he was aware of hers for him. Above all he wanted to spare Virgie. He did his best. But there was no deceiving Virgie. She's like a fox. She spied, she knew everything there was to know about her father. She loved him. She hated him—for my sake."

"But, Alex," I said, and could not help my tone, "after all these years when you might have divorced Hal or simply decided to leave him in Steepleton and live somewhere else, why—can you tell me?—why did you finally resort to this extreme? You're a sensible woman. Why did you finally give way?"

"Oh," she said, "one afternoon—not long ago—we were riding back alone in silence. Side by side. Suddenly he reined in and looked at me. 'You know,' he said, 'I have come to a conclusion. I am no longer interested in other women. Too bad you didn't give me a good kick long ago. But have you noticed that I've stopped drinking? I think it's time that you and I started living.'

"That," Alex said to me, quickening a little, "that's when I was affronted. My years of sacrifice, his mistress, his women, his girls, and now it meant nothing. As if when I had crossed the fifty line and he his sixtieth he could just sit there in the sunset and change his mind. 'Start living'! Yes, it was then that I was affronted, that I was struck dumb with insult. I smiled with rage. I knew absolutely what to do. Oh, wouldn't I give him a good kick!"

She stopped. Alex in bed, wearing only a silk peignoir the shell-pink color of pure desire, this Alex had just made the speech of her life without intending to. She was breathless, surprised and satisfied. We understood that the speech she might have made to Hal she had just made to me. That's how much I was favored.

Her breathing grew even, she drew up the wisp of silk on her shoulder. She was relieved, secure, her own woman. And already thinking of other things. She looked anything but unwell.

"More questions?" she asked.

I shook my head.

"Comments?"

I had none. I could not tell her that at that moment, half of her head of auburn hair lit by the light of the reading lamp, the other half a deeper red in the darkness, she reminded me of the oil painting of the sleeping wife and betrayed husband on the dining room wall back to back with Whistlejacket. But I was neither the betrayed husband nor the young author of the letter plucked from the smiling wife's still fingers. I had never noticed the combination of Alex's age—fifty-two is not the same thing as thirty or even forty-five—and her womanly appearance. Yet Alex, I thought standing up, was the one woman denied me, not by age but by convention. Was there any woman as much my mother as Alex?

I put my tray outside in the corridor, did the same with the other.

"Mike," she said, as I turned to close her door, "come back a moment."

I stepped inside, the door clicked shut behind me.

"I want to show you my love letters."

She couldn't mean what she had just said, I thought. After this day and night? Impossible.

"Alex," I said, "you're not serious."

"I'm always serious. You know that."

"But love letters? Now?"

"Well, do you want to see them?"

"Of course I do," I said. She had already made me her accomplice. Now this.

She told me where to look. In a scented drawer between two layers of lingerie, silk shapelessness which I probed like the guiltiest of intruders. Limp shoulder straps attached to nothing. Scalloped edges laced together in seamless skins.

A pair of panties identified itself, slipped over the back of my hand. Then I touched what I wanted.

Again I sat beside Alex.

"Well? Go on, open it."

I lifted the flap, from that envelope drew out the sheaf tied, as such packets always are, with a ribbon.

"But, Alex," I said, "these aren't letters. They're photographs."

"Oh, well," she said, "that's what I call them. They're from Hal."

I leaned toward Alex and saw that each of the photographs was like the next. Polaroids. Poor color. A man, a woman. Nude. Variations on the familiar position of standing man and kneeling woman. Sometimes the woman's hair was short, sometimes long, sometimes the long hair was down and at others hastily tied up. There was a full-length mirror, the man was taking the photographs by aiming into the mirror, though occasionally he had simply pointed the camera down at the top of the woman's head.

I glanced at Alex, back to the Polaroids, took a breath. Turned from photograph to photograph more slowly. The man was generally identifiable as Hal. But the pictures were blurred, the woman harder to see. Because Hal and the woman were not acting, and because the dull color of the surfaces of the pictures glistened as brightly as the bodies of Hal and his partners.

"Hal," I said. "And you?"

"Not in every one. Me. Buse. Some of his girls."

"But, Alex," I said, "you let him take your picture this way?"

"You can believe what you see. These were taken over several years. We only looked together at the ones of himself and me. Then one day he gave me the whole batch."

"I didn't know he took Polaroids," I said.

"You could do better."

"Not my kind of work," I said.

"Why don't you take them along?" she said. "But bring them back."

How did she know the nervous young photographer that well? What intuition prompted her to offer exactly what I wanted but never would have suggested? That remark of hers puzzled yet pleased me even more than the Polaroids themselves. Nonetheless I stood up, my back to her, and put the pictures in the envelope and stuffed it into my pocket.

At the door I turned and tried to save face. "Love letters!" I said, and laughed.

I noticed a silky overflow hanging from the open drawer. I escaped.

As I saw the following morning, Alex had had no trouble sleeping, had not accompanied my wakefulness with hers. She was fresher than ever, as if the previous day and her hours with me had not occurred. We met at the usual time in the kitchen—no matter how much or little I sleep my arising time does not vary—and while we ate, she casually announced that I was to move into Hal's former rooms. They could not remain unoccupied, she said, and would not do for guests, whereas my own rooms were appropriate for guests, especially for older single men or married couples.

"Married?" I said, but she was already getting up from the table.

A day or two at most, I decided, and concentrated on the practicalities rather than the significance of the move. Yet it was obvious that I, not Alex, was packing up Hal's effects and that I had been manipulated into taking Hal's place in one sense or another. Again Alex was making the choices, I doing the work. Well, perhaps I would not return her Polaroids unless she asked for them.

I cleared my equipment from Hal's apartment, brought down from the top floor of Steepleton, which was devoted entirely to storage, cartons, empty trunks, Hal's own set of leather valises. Newspaper, white tissue, cord. Small plastic sacks from the kitchen. I threw nothing out, saved it all. I went quickly but also with care, methodically devising categories, such as suits with suits, riding clothes in separate suitcases, and so forth, before emptying bureau, closets, desk. I swathed the wooden horse in tissue, gave it a separate carton. And I labeled the cartons. H. O. Van Fleet might only have been setting off to relocate in England, say, or better still in Ireland, where horses are more beloved than people.

Item by item I piled it all against the wall in the corridor until nothing personal remained in what had been Hal's rooms. Except one photograph. A single photograph I had left on Hal's bureau top for the weeks I had spent in his rooms professionally, so to speak, and for the few days it took me to clear those rooms of all but the furniture. A prize I had turned my back on until now, saving it for myself. I had known vaguely that I wanted to take it down to the darkroom for copying. But I had driven it from mind, had saved it for last. For myself. It was a large sepia-tinted photograph in a black wooden frame, twelve or fourteen inches wide yet not disproportionate to the top of the bureau. It faced the foot and hence the entire length of Hal's bed. Propped comfortably on his mass of white pillows, he could stare at the photograph, the only one that pleased him, whenever he wished.

A horse and rider filled the entire lower half of that photograph. Hal, of course, and a dark, heavy hunter named Raconteur. Horse and rider sharply in profile. A noble pair. Hal in hunting clothes at about the time of his marriage, Raconteur staring straight ahead as if into history. No other photograph showed to such advantage Hal's lifted head, long, unsmiling face, straight shoulders, and, best of all, the swooping, exaggerated inward sway of his back.

Finished. Except for the photograph. I sat on the end of the bed in which I would sleep that night and looked up at the famous photograph of Hal. It was only days before the memorial hunt, when the guests would arrive, filling our driveway and the cobbled stableyard with their horse vans and trailers, and laughing and telling loud stories throughout the four nights that Alex had invited them to stay. But for now silence. Settling dust. The last traces of Hal removed. Except for the swaybacked man on the bold horse.

I crossed to the bureau, picked up the photograph, wiped its glass with my handkerchief. It had been deliberately aged by the photographer, thanks mainly to a background made entirely of simulated clouds. Horse and rider removed from time and photographed in no place that ever existed. I shook my head in admiration. There was a small black dog between the horse's front legs, a flask in a leather case affixed by brass snaps to the saddle. His stern expression. Harold O. Van Fleet himself.

Suddenly, on impulse, I turned over that photograph, looked closely at the brown wrinkling paper that was glued to the frame. And as I knew before I looked, Hal's portrait had been tampered with. The backing had been cut, opened, pasted in place again. But not by a person meddling in Hal's affairs, trying to do him harm. No, I thought, it had been Hal himself. Hal's own secretive act. But why? To hide something, for as long as the framed photograph existed, and clearly Hal had assumed that such a portrait of himself would be passed on, reverently, to stand on this tabletop or hang on that wall forever. But what could he have hidden? A real letter? Several letters folded out flat and secreted between the photograph and its backing? Perhaps Alex and I had been wrong about Hal. Perhaps there had been an unknown woman after all.

I took the photograph down to the darkroom and on a cleared white Formica surface removed the backing. No letter, as I should have known, but a second photograph. Nearly as large as the portrait concealing it, and for a moment I thought Hal himself had been the photographer. Black and white, grainy. Innocent and clandestine both. "Two Ladies in the Woods of Steepleton," read the caption he had written with pen and ink on the reverse side. In caption and quality here was the unmistakable twin to "A Tangle of Limbs." Yet the one was only a snapshot whereas the other was an ambitious act of photography. Similarly capricious, similarly erotic, twins at first glance, but different. How had Hal directed the photographer so that the final results bore so close a resemblance to Hal's own foray into the life of the camera—excluding the Polaroids, that is? I would never know.

But like "A Tangle of Limbs," "Two Ladies in the Woods of Steepleton" is now mine. It hangs in my studio-loft in town.

Somehow Hal had gotten hold of an antique black limousine and, accompanied by his two subjects and the photographer, had driven into the woods on an abandoned dirt road chopped and torn by endless processions of horses with sharp hooves. He had swung the limousine off the road and into the speckling light under the trees. He and the two women had drunk champagne, the women—laughing—had undressed. Completely. The photographer was behind his camera and tripod, black hood over his head.

The rear door on the viewer's side of the limousine is open, the women stand side by side and hold each other about the waists. Their heads are close together; the left legs are raised, feet propped on the running board. Each woman appears to be standing on a single leg. The women are at ease, the head of the woman on the right is turned toward her companion so that the left-hand side of her face is visible. But the woman on the left has turned her face only far enough to catch the eyes of the other so that nothing but a sliver of her face is visible. The woman on the left, the one with the shorter hair, is more slender than the widely smiling woman on her right. The woman on the right is the heavier and the more girlish, though she is not younger. The bodies of both women are smudged where the flexed muscles and looser flesh create shadows as dark as the trees and leaves and limousine itself. The trimmer body, the heavier body, the shapes that cannot be matched by the male form, the natural focus on the women's buttocks, different from woman to woman yet unmistakably female—both women have their appeal, their attractiveness, their erotic lure, though taste might assign priorities.

The women are standing straight, holding and looking at each other with the intimacy only they could share. But they are about to stoop and disappear forever into the limousine, where Hal awaits them. The photographer, who preserved for Hal this afternoon in the woods, sits on a stump and bides his time for the return of ordinary life as he knows it.

Alex and Buse? Shortly after the permanent arrival of Hal's mistress? Yes, the one on the right, the plumper one, is finally recognizable as Buse. But about the woman on the left it's impossible to say. I tell myself that she is Alex. I could ask her, of course, but I won't.

How long did I first look at that photograph? I don't know. But suddenly I raised my head, listened to my silent voice. Did Alex really want me to take pictures of the sort Hal had snapped of her? Only better? Did she want to spend hours nude in the very studio she had had built for my work on Hal?

Whenever she wished, I thought. Then I concealed "Two Women in the Woods of Steepleton" where I had found it and took it back up to my new apartment. Later I would rephotograph Hal on his horse. Later.

The next morning Alex did not appear for breakfast. I waited awhile for Buse, for Virgie. No one. So after eating—I had slept long and well—I started down hoping to find one or all of them in the stable.

A warmer day, hard light. A breeze. Halfway to the arch I stopped as Harry emerged from it leading a horse. Marcabru. Neck long, head lowered, taking slow strides, docile, he was hardly recognizable as the same horse. The breeze stirred his long mane and tail.

"The vet been here?" I called.

Harry swung Marcabru sideways, posed him for me.

"That's right," Harry called back, "the vet's been here. What do you think of our killer?" Harry was laughing. "Like a lamb, eh? Like a lamb!"

"Those films of mine are still missing."

"I know they are."

"But you didn't take them, Alex."

"No. It was Virgie."

"Virgie's got them?"

"No. Harry's got them. But he doesn't know he does."

"Alex. I want those films."

"Well, Harry did the photography. His pictures were the ones you found scratched up."

"He mutilated his own films?"

"That was Virgie."

"Alex, just tell me what happened."

"Harry took two rolls, hid one, and sent the other off for developing."

"Why?"

"Oh, he wanted to be part of things. But he really wanted something to hold over us."

"A blackmailer."

"Just to hold over us."

"Money?"

"Ourselves. He's gotten nothing from Virgie or me so far. Though I'm not so sure about Virgie."

"Go on, Alex."

"Virgie pilfered Harry's developed film. What could he do? Besides, he still thinks he has the original. But he doesn't. He has yours. Virgie had already substituted one of your rolls for Harry's original and kept the original. Always meaning to destroy it."

"Alex. I developed two rolls of film."

"Harry's original plus one of your own."

"Which means that in the drying process, when I went back up to my rooms, Virgie scratched the remaining original roll of Harry's films, which I had developed, and substituted her own nearly obliterated films for my own and then went off with mine. So Harry has an undeveloped roll of my film, I have two rolls of his pictures developed and disfigured, and Virgie's got half my developed films."

"I don't have the mind you do," said Alex. "Anyway, you better leave well enough alone."

"So what I want doesn't matter."

"Of course it does. To me."

12

EXCEPT FOR CAROL—Carol has always stood apart from the photographers' models I have known and know—Susan is the most suited for rearview portraits. After my run on mouths I did a spate of them.

Bonnie, Sylvia, and Susan are all about the same size. Large. Big girls, as Alice says. From any view—the front, the side, three-quarters, the full rear—Bonnie is not to be compared with Sylvia or Susan. Bonnie, despite her size, has nothing of the solidity of the other two, nothing of the Nordic maturity implicit in the large, hard, womanly bodies of her professional sisters. Compared with Susan and Sylvia, Bonnie is still on the last edge of adolescence, which is to say agreeable, receptive, naive, soft. All the largeness of her body is soft. She is the permanent virgin, no matter how often she protests and even demonstrates the opposite. Why else would Alice select her for an assignment? Susan, Sylvia, and Bonnie are all the same age. Young. Carol is the model I photograph most often, Bonnie the least.

After my success with Ashley, whose puckered mouth sent me on to mouths, I flew off to an island hideaway with Bonnie. The beach, Alice said. Tropical light. So I photographed Bonnie squatting on the beach in colors too bright for anyone except young women interested in buying tasteless clothes. A cut below my work with Ashley. But I did it.

A single working day on the beach. Dawn and dusk. A single day. We had only the few hours of the first sun and the last since the rest of the day was lit by sunlight too intense for color. But at dawn and dusk we found our parrot-feather light that Alice's clients wanted. The tropical light, my choice of filters, the clothes. Pale blue pants rolled up at the cuff, yellow stretch top, the softest possible white and yellowish shirt patterned with tiny flowers and worn with the sleeves folded high and the front tails tied so that a single twisted bunny's ear of the thin cloth hung down between the spread knees—the photograph finally chosen could not have been more garish.

I settled on the obvious colors, rose and purple. Bonnie fills the picture, she squats on the toes of bare feet, her hands droop between her lazy knees, and her fingers pick at a few violet flowers of the fat lei hanging from hands to wet sand then trailing to the right, where it sharply disappears off the edge of the picture. It is a fat lei that hides the toes— in a picture such as this one the toes are taboo—and the beach sweeps up to the right in a faintly purple swath cut by the blur of warm foamy water, which, out of focus, makes a lightening pattern on the reddish purple sand. Bonnie's hair is wet, stringy, parted low on the left side of her head, and brushed in a long heap up and over and back.

I did my best with this picture. A fragment of coral, actually white foam on the beach, is just visible and looks like an earring trapped between her right earlobe and girlish cheek. Bonnie's fingers are fiddling with the flowers, her elbow to the viewer's right has been dipped in sand and leaves a thin line of sand on the broad right knee, which, like the other, cushions one of her forearms. With no effort she squats up on the toes of her strong feet in that violet light. The roundish sentimental face is turned slightly to the right—my left—and her smile is faint, the hazel eyes look at me, the photographer, where I am crouching somewhat to her left—my right—which is to say that the eyes are not looking in the same direction as the face itself. In this picture

Bonnie is alone. Her boyfriend is back home, the picture says, and it is into her boyfriend's eyes that the fictional Bonnie is looking. The rising or perhaps setting sun brightens the right-hand side of her face.

It is just as easy to make a lei in the Caribbean, where we were, as it is in Honolulu, though the lei insists to the picture's intended viewers that this innocent young girl's lonely world is Honolulu. Her clothes appear to be fresh off the rack. But the pants are tight, the pale blue calves bulge, tight wrinkles make half rings down the left-hand curve of the blue mass that is thigh and lower buttock all in one. To my eye at least.

As soon as I knew that I had taken this photograph—the wan and sentimental and hence totally unreal photograph that Alice's clients would buy—I told Bonnie that I wanted her to destroy the clothes.

She was baffled but obliging as always.

I told her to lie down with about half her body, her right-side, in the water. I began to use first one then the other camera. I told her to rub herself into the sand, to stand up with legs spread and, facing away from me, to bend from the waist, touching her toes. Then to untie the shirt, to pull it off one shoulder, to lie facedown in the sand. Pull one knee to her chest, raising her bottom like a sprinter getting ready to run. Now to run off, arms outflung—she objected—I told her to run. I took more photographs. She returned out of breath, covered in sand. So I told her to run into the water shoulder-high, to come back to the beach, to lie face upwards and pull her knees to her chest. She was laughing. Then up onto hands and knees, I said, head hanging, then chest to the sand, knees widespread, head on hands in the foam, elbows wide, buttocks high.

She perspired, complained, her makeup disappeared, a seam ripped, her hair hung flat to her skull, she dropped the shirt and stretch top to the beach as I told her to—they were gone the next morning—and then, still laughing, covered her breasts with hands or arms until I tossed her a towel. But I was not playing as Bonnie was. And I was indifferent to Bonnie's modesty. I saw nothing but the potential of rearview photographs lying ahead.

* * *

I resent the photographer who attempts to disguise or even obliterate a model's buttocks, as many do, by using light and angle to flatten the surface of this tight undergarment or that. I do not take such photographs, no matter the fashion. Anyone who has seriously portrayed the woman's body from the rear knows what it is to become absorbed in the buttocks—spoken together in the plural but conceived in the singular—as undisputed physical and erotic center of the woman's body. The hips frame the buttocks and become them, the buttocks subsume the woman's weight but also her sex. Size, shape, above all proximity account for the erotic power of the buttocks. A woman's sex is easily concealed. The same claim cannot be made for the buttocks.

Like most of us, I am offended by euphemism and vulgarism alike. And yet the difficulty of translating the plural—"buttocks"—into a singular form tends to compel the speaker into one language camp or the other. "Seat," "bottom," "behind," or "ass" or "arse" or *derrière*—the force that detonates resistance to such words is lack of equivalency. Practice doesn't make for ease, usually they're spoken defensively, uncomfortably, self-consciously. They designate but never evoke their anatomical referent. Breasts fare better than buttocks. The singular of "buttocks" does not exist—in any usable form.

An example is Boucher's "Mademoiselle O'Murphy"—I prefer Miss O'Murphy—the famous painting of the child mistress of Louis XV. The plump girl lies on a couch on her stomach, torso raised, head propped on folded hands, which in turn rest on the vertical then sharply curving end of the couch. She is nude, her legs are spread, the right is lifted at the knee and rests on an immense and nearly upright pillow all puffs and shadows, while the other leg, the one closest the viewer—and this is the masterstroke— lies half fallen from the couch so as to draw the eye from childish leg to hidden sex to Miss O'Murphy's bottom. Her little face is prim, her hair is coiled atop her head. She lies on a rumpled sheet, the pinkness and softness of her body are so tinted and brightened that though this child looks straight ahead and parts her tiny lips—not for speech—still Miss O'Murphy's bottom is all that matters. One glimpse and the viewer has little interest in the rest of that plump body. Why? Because of the left leg. It is fallen into its wanton effect. But more, this suggestive position lifts the opposite or far buttock just enough to silhouette it against the dark paneling behind the couch. The decorum of the little face, the nudeness, the lowered leg, the small buttock in relief—and there is not one descriptive term, including bottom, that is worthy of the concentrated plumpness that makes Miss O'Murphy even more desirable than the woman she will grow to be. Thanks to her bare buttocks she was assured her place in art and history. And the noun for it all is missing.

Most of us, trapped among commonplace expressions, try metaphor or search for the euphemism not yet clichéd. Hal's "croup," for instance, or, more surprising and hyperbolic, his coinage of "bowl of wine." There is the medieval phrase of "cheeks of the winds." Or the valentine which, familiarly enough, combines the heart and buttocks. "Fanny" is a word spoken only by women. A French lexicographer has compiled a collection of twenty-five slang words and phrases in his native tongue, amusing to his friends but useless, even in translation, to anyone with a serious aesthetic-anatomical interest in women.

"Buttocks" is the ugliest word of them all yet is the most concrete. I avoid metaphor and use the others as sparingly as possible. I prefer the concrete.

I could do nothing with the rearview photographs I took of Bonnie in the Caribbean except keep them—to myself, that is. They did justice neither to my abilities nor to the potential of the woman's body seen not as it faces the camera but turns away. I destroyed the negatives, kept one set of enlargements, which I showed to no one—discounting Alice. Alice and I shared those photographs for a half hour one afternoon. But she saw in them what I hoped she might, and so it was thanks to Alice that the progression of photographs I wanted to do next was not accidental as in Bonnie's case. Swift, obsessive, requiring three weeks or five, intuitive or carefully planned—whatever they were, they were not accidental but rather conveyed the will of the photographer as much as the lure of his subject.

Anyone looking at the photographs that followed my half hour face-to-face or side-by-side with Alice—usually we limit ourselves to a minimum number of words on the telephone—would naturally assume that a different model appears in each. Yet Susan posed for them all. Alice made Susan possible, Susan made the pictures possible.

In the sauna, for instance. A shaft of sunlight as orange as the stripped logs, the blond wooden bench, the tall nude woman bending over, back to the camera, and drying an invisible foot raised to the bench. The light is so deeply orange that for one instant the viewer does not register what's on the retina—the size and smoothness of the buttocks. Or another photograph of a large woman lying nude in the dawn light on a towel spread on the gray planks of an unstable quay. The camera is directly in front of her and pointed down. Not directly down but down. She looks up, turtle fashion, eyes hidden behind black sunglasses, black hair bound in a ribbon. The upraised face is not a face, the camera's line of sight skims it, rests on the buttocks. Her body is oiled, her buttocks could not be mistaken for a man's. Then there is my version of a hot woods, a woman wearing a brown homemade dress, nothing more, and seated on a stone wall. A three-quarters' view from the rear, the mid-thigh dress tight to the body, half unzipped down the back. Shoulder straps. The face is expressionless, the black hair oiled and tousled, the hands crossed at the waist. She leans forward. Her left hand, which is nearest the camera, makes a fist and tightens the brown cotton across the heavy thigh as far as the buttocks. The dress scoops open in the back, pops open in front, revealing a portion of her right breast. Large. The breast is analogous to the mass of the buttocks. The eye oscillates, comes to rest.

I lost sight of the various contexts in which her body was bared, covered, always shown. Sometimes she was faceless, sometimes not. Down we went on road after new road toward what I could see and she could feel with two hands held behind her back palms inward.

Then came a diversion, a challenge, which was to celebrate a new style of women's open- and high-heeled shoe. Only a shoe when I could think of nothing but rear views. How, I wondered, could I manipulate the viewer's eye to see a shoe—mere shoe—as never before? How put a shoe, which is insignificant compared with a woman's body, in the center of a photograph where it does not belong? One piece of jewelry can dominate face, thighs, buttocks of a model even as large and original-looking as Susan. Not so the shoe.

Yet it was precisely my insistence on rear views that solved the problem.

This photograph—I am proud of it—depends on a blond wooden floor still deeper gold in the light I gave it, and on a heavy modern table of a wood stained a red-gold color to match the floor, and on totally black shadow at the far end of the picture. Susan is dressed for early evening in a short red jersey skirt, a black patent leather belt, the shoes I meant to exalt. But if I had not had Susan's height and weight to work with, I would not have been able to create this photograph. Only a young woman as tall as Susan could have rested all her weight on her right shin on the edge of the massive table and allowed her left leg to hang to the floor—toe all but touching—without appearing grotesque. But so she poses, Susan leaning on one half-bared leg and on her elbows, hands clasped, torso horizontal to the tabletop and face turned to the viewer. Light and model work together, her black hair disappears into the geometric blackness of the shadow, half her face is as white as the shoulder blades emerging from the V in her black off-the-shoulder top. The red skirt rides to mid-thigh and in its surrounding black and gold dominates the picture. But the famous shoes? In the center of this nearly abstract portrait. Where else? Or one of them is.

The bent right leg—most of the long shin is concealed by shadow and the wedge of red skirt—necessitates that the right foot lie with its heel tucked into the bottom of Susan's bowl of wine, most of the foot and all of the heelless shoe silhouetted against the broad round golden edge of the table and fixed forever to the elegant color inseparable from Susan's seat.

It is an erotic photograph to any viewer of exceptional eye. No one could find it vulgar. Yet there's no denying that in its composition the eye has nowhere to go but to the tailored red cloth drawn tight around the buttocks, and so to the shoe. One fetish celebrates another.

Women want to see what they think men want to see. Why not?

13

ALEXANDRA WAS DETERMINED to begin the three days devoted to Hal's memory with a ritual called the Blessing of the Hounds.

I pointed out that we had already had a Blessing of the Hounds, that Hal himself had, as always, presided over the age-old tradition requiring that for the well-being of all, men and hounds alike, the hounds be blessed at the start of the yearly fox hunting season. One Blessing, I said, was enough. There was something ill-fated about a second, especially since her own husband, so recently alive and vigorous, had called the first into being. Still, in her own gentle way she persisted and in passing reminded me that I was not to tell her what to do. She had had enough of that, she said, and would let me know if she wished it otherwise.

Alex had invited so many guests that there were horse vans and horse trailers everywhere, parked haphazardly on lawns and in gardens which, dormant and withered now, nonetheless deserved better than the heavy tires, the sharp hooves of disembarking horses, the thoughtless trampling of horse people gathered to solemnize Hal's death. Horse vans, horse trailers, limousines—one like a white armored car belonged to Charlie Madden, a little man ten years' Hal's senior but his closest friend—and pickup trucks and heavy-duty trucks and other vehicles as long and sleek as submarines—they had all arrived, the hickory fires were lit in Steepleton, mists and cold air came down. Then freezing rain.

In intermittent freezing rain we gathered on that first morning, thirty or forty riders in canary britches, white stocks, generally black coats and black top hats. Woodsmoke and cold wet air, the heavy sounds of horses crowding the stables, some already being walked up and down in rain sheets. The priest, not the Episcopalian who had officiated at Hal's funeral, as I had feared, but a Catholic, came down with Alex and took his place in the cobblestone stableyard where the formal assembly was held.

"A female MFH!" cried Charlie Madden, catching hold of my arm. "Travesty!"

I too was surprised to see Alex wearing the red coat and black hunting cap reserved for the Master of Foxhounds. But I was concerned about more than custom, and what of the black armband she was wearing? Was it possible for Alexandra to mourn? Or, more difficult still, to feign the grief appropriate to Hal's widow?

"And look at that!" cried Charlie under his breath—he was as small as a jockey yet had a bass voice that startled anyone who didn't know him, especially women. "Isn't that the poor devil's horse? What's happened to him? What's she doing? Why, you'd think this was the National Cemetery."

"You're right, Charlie," I said. "It's Hal's horse."

"Gelded," said Charlie.

I nodded.

"Perfectly good stallion," said Charlie, standing not as tall as my shoulder and booming away like a big fellow on a stage, though as softly as he could, "but it's inappropriate to have that horse around this morning. And look at me. Red coat, brass horn. Alex insists I join this travesty. Hal would turn over, as they say."

We laughed, I shivered at the sight of Virgie holding Marcabru in a far corner, the large horse framed in stone glistening and white from ice and rain. Marcabru was saddled, his stirrup irons were raised, the reins were looped back and held under them. He wore black crepe. A horse forever without a rider.

"Still," I said, smelling Charlie's breath—whiskey—"it's a sad day."

"Can't be anything else," said Charlie. "But she's enjoying herself. Looks better, now that he's gone."

Then he patted my arm and pushed off into the crowd toward the space where Alex and the priest and five other red-coated men stood waiting with large brass hunting horns slung sideways over their heads and across their chests.

The previous night, when arriving guests were weary and expectant both, Virgie had introduced me to the only friend she had among all those come to pay homage to Harold O. Van Fleet. The friend, Brownie Lupton, was a quick-eyed girl neither large nor plump yet somehow tight in her skin, and had only one interest according to Virgie—men. Virgie was pleased that her friend had come. I was pleased that Virgie finally had a friend, no matter how young. Now I looked about, trying to find her in the crowd. No luck.

"I know who you're looking for," said a voice at my back, "but you better keep away from that girl."

"Buse," I said, putting my arm around her waist, "she's not for me. Besides, Charlie Madden has already put the moves, as they say, on Brownie Lupton."

"She's pretty cute," said Buse.

"Not exactly my word," I said.

Again I saw how much weight Buse had lost, though she would always be heavyset, and how forlorn she had become since Hal's death.

"All these people," she said, surprising me as she did now and again, "might have been at his funeral. That would have been better."

I leaned down, kissed her cheek. And before we could say more, Charlie stiffened and the first burst of Latin sounded, shocking the entire group into silence. No one had thought much about the priest and there was no reason to think that he would do anything other than bow his head and intone the usual short prayer hard to hear and impossible to understand. But not this priest. His robes were wet through, he had been rightly judged as shabby and having no place at Steepleton. Nonetheless his voice was strong and with his loud voice alone he achieved silence and even respect. As for the Latin, the clarity and aggression with which it rose into that cold air and through the rain conveyed its message, the very sound of it becoming sense, as if the priest were in a cathedral and his chant rising toward the highest winged creatures carved in stone. Another and longer burst half an octave higher and still strong enough to make monks hang their heads and flowers appear in a cold nave. He was angry, he had become a large and portentous spirit instead of a stooping, poor-looking priest, and Marcabru shied and a few hounds on leashes began to bay.

On the heels of the prayers came the horns. Buse shivered against me, the Latin ended abruptly, the horns struck up the note the priest had just abandoned. He had so consumed our attention that I had not been aware of the crescent of red-coated men ducking their heads and extricating themselves from the brass horns each fashioned in a single large loop and in diameter expanding from the size of a finger into the width of the bell so broad across that it required being held on the hip. The priest had been in command of his Latin, but now the players were in command of their horns. One long cadenza, another, the bodies and breath of the red-coated men became the music of kings, of the hunt in full regalia, of heavenly choirs. Louder and louder—Charlie Madden, flushed and trembling, rigid and struggling to hold his large horn, looked as if he might topple at any moment, starved for air, starved for blood, victim of strain—and higher and higher, on and on it went, this chorale of brass, this pealing across hills and fields and ages of the hunt.

Suddenly with a flourish it stopped.

"My God," said a man at my elbow, "I'm glad that's over."

"If there's ever been a Blessing," said a portly man in a bowler and checked jacket, "that was it."

Then confusion, hounds underfoot, relief, the priest exiting, a general rush to the horses as servants brought trays of liquor and wine.

"Where's that girl?" said Charlie Madden, red-faced, again at my side.

"Don't worry, Charlie," I said, "you'll find her. Incidentally, I didn't know you're an expert on the horn."

"Thought I'd die."

In another twenty minutes or so, and led by Alex on Lady Di, we started off. The day, all three days in fact, were to be devoted to the pursuit of the real fox instead of the mere scent of a gunnysack splashed with fox urine and dragged about the countryside for the hounds to follow. For our occasion Alex had imported live foxes, which were long gone from the environs of Steepleton, and one had been loosed much earlier and with plenty of time to make the chase difficult for the hounds, while another was being held in readiness in case the first outwitted our hounds and escaped, thereby ruining the day for hounds and riders alike.

"She's using the bitch pack," said Harry Martin, suddenly beside me and just as suddenly gone. "It'll be a good day if there's any scent!"

Up ahead, her big chestnut wedged between the horses of the portly man and another I recognized as a banker friend of Hal's, rode Brownie Lupton, rising and falling to the trot, head turning to the man in the checked jacket on her left, the man on her right. I pressed forward.

But Pretty Polly, the Lupton girl's sweet chestnut as Alex had said, when in fact the horse was far from sweet since it wore a red ribbon tied to the tip of its tail—a horse that kicked, the ribbon warned—popped from between the mounts of the portly man and the banker and cantered off. The abandoned men made no attempt to follow but instead closed up the space the girl had left, just as the road narrowed and the dense trees crowded in on either side of us.

I pulled up, thinking that Harry was right and that it would be a good day's chase. There were frozen ruts in the road and again the rain was driving down, hard going for little Martha, a fine-boned chestnut nearly auburn in comparison to Polly's great splash of reddish gold, nonetheless she danced along at a nice trot, despite the sluggish pace of the horses blocking our way. I was making an effort to hold her straight—Martha's only fault was sometimes to walk or trot or canter crookedly with the forward part of her trim body slewing to the right of the rear—and from far off I heard the faint blasts of Jim West's horn—West had been Hal's huntsman for years—which told us all that the hounds had picked up the line, or scent, and that our fox was running. Alex, who carried a horn as small and efficient as her huntsman's, for of course Jim West was now Alexandra's huntsman, would be riding hard where she could see and be seen, and as the banker and his portly acquaintance stopped talking about Brownie Lupton and broke into a lumbering canter, suddenly I thought of the day Alex had given me a soft-spoken lecture on the superiority of mares over geldings.

I could not place the day, it was a brief episode I had forgotten until now when all the sounds of the chase came drifting back to the three of us who for some reason were still caught in the confining woods. But clearly I remembered Alex's brief praise of mares.

Mares, she said, had not been altered, in them the blood flowed freely, their life cycles had not been tampered with, their natures were completely their own. The mare usually had more energy then the gelding, could be as temperamental as the stallion and was, in fact, its superior. The mare had lent her name to the nightmare, boats and ships were referred to as "she" because they bobbed and sailed the seas like mares. Buy a mare whenever you need a horse, Alex had said, her pride in the female horse's gender as admirable, I thought, as her love of music. Lady Di, Misty Rose, Martha—all were mares and not, I realized, by accident.

A bend in the road, an opening off to the right through a stand of birches, and I saw my chance and squeezed my legs around Martha's girth, and in another moment we were alone on a broad ridge and running flat-out. It was slippery footing yet I saw no serious obstacles and thought I knew that we were headed in the right direction. But then an unavoidable mass of oaks, a gate someone had left open—

it was an offense serious enough to warrant being sent home from the field—and once through it I spent precious moments shutting that unruly gate.

"I've lost my way!" came a girl's voice, and there, suddenly, was Brownie Lupton on the chestnut mare, rider and horse as still as a statue on a village green.

"Me too!" I called, but she wheeled about, the red bow on Polly's tail whipping the air, and instead of waiting for me, as naturally I thought she would, she merely charged off through the underbrush, ice and dead branches shattering beneath her horse's hooves.

Martha was faster, I thought, than the big chestnut, and there was no mistaking the trail that the plunging horse and laughing girl left behind. Yet by the time I had escaped from the trees and tangles of briar looming up directly in the path Polly and Brownie must have taken, the girl and her willful horse had disappeared.

I broke into the clear, thoroughly turned around, but drove straight at my first jump of the morning, a chicken coop, so called, that covered strands of barbed wire, and Martha took the jump with her hooves tucked up and, on landing and of her own accord, swerved to the right, where along the crest of a low hill streamed hounds and riders. Mistakenly I decided that it was best to try to catch up with them downfield and so turned Martha to the left and toward a low stone wall. We jumped it. And avoided an old rusty hay rake that sat abandoned in the middle of the field.

"Huntsman wanted! Huntsman wanted!" came a lone voice, a woman's, from somewhere far to my left, and I turned more sharply still.

I heard Martha's breathing, that urgent watery sound in throat and nostrils, I thought that most of the morning's riders must have become as separated from the hunt as myself.

Then I saw the fox.

I had slowed Martha to a trot and was going along reasonably, safely, pleased to spare Martha and myself from exhaustion, when I saw the fox. In total silence, less than a hundred yards ahead, there he was, cutting across my path at an indifferent pace. I reined in, I watched, I stared at the dark red color of our quarry against the frozen whitish stubble in which we two alone existed. He struck me as old, he had survived many a hound and many a riotous sports- man and frothing horse, he gave me hardly a glance, intu- iting that I was not the sort of rider to raise a hue and cry or start after him. By the end of the day he would be driven to ground and torn by the Van Fleet hounds until one of the whippers-in, Harry Martin or Charlie Madden or someone else, leapt from his horse and drove them off, then out of the chaos held up his brush and head, while the hounds yelped and the riders crowded around. But for now he was free and taking his time, sparing himself as I was, crossing the field without a thought, it seemed, for the thirty-six bitches that were hot after him, plainly visible and only a field away as I saw then, twisting in my saddle and watching as the string of hounds bore down on us, well on the scent, no matter the bad day, and without another horseman in sight.

"Careful," I admonished the old fox. Martha was hardly able to contain herself beneath me and the bitches in a long, slow arc were starting to leap the rock wall dividing the fields. "Careful, don't press your luck!"

Until the last moment the large red fox played his part, confident that he was swifter than the thirty-six hounds and more elusive than any fox the Van Fleet pack had pursued so far. He did not know this countryside and yet had caught his breath, had already devised his plan to throw the eager bitches off the scent and find the copse, the overlay of branch and bramble where he would wait, flat on his belly, until he could safely emerge and trot off in the other direction.

Martha tossed her head, champed on the bit. Overhead a single crow might have been signaling the fox. I thought that perhaps he would start away slowly, gain speed, and that I would be able to watch the lean, shaggy-coated old animal speeding away, bitches behind him like the tail of a kite. But the bitches all at once and all together threw their tongues and their burst of music was louder than I had expected— they were that close—and Fairmaid, Frisky, Clio, Bonny, Gaylass, Sappho and the rest of them leapt forward, mad- eyed, ribs showing, and in a brown-and-white mass, wet and steaming, came between myself and the fox. Then on, strung out again, still on the line, without even a streak of red in the distance to hold my eye. He was gone, out from under their teeth and noses. He had not been buried in that tumble of dogs, had not been caught. Not yet.

Horsemen began to appear from all directions as swiftly as the hounds had sung and raced on. Jim West was at my elbow, reining in, while I, bareheaded and holding my cap at arm's length, pointed the way, as he who has last seen the fox is obliged to do. We were wet, Jim's face was red, but instead of simply raising horn to lips and sending forth his own huntsman's cry and riding without hesitation in pursuit of the by now invisible hounds, he stopped, spoke a few words.

"Back there," he said, catching his breath, "I saw an old fellow crossing a field and stopped and asked him if he'd seen the fox. He shook his head then said he hadn't seen him but that his wife had dreamt she saw him the other night. Then he sent me in the wrong direction!"

I laughed and pointed again with my cap.

"Mike," Jim said, "cover your head. I know where that fox is!"

But it so happened that I had pointed the entire lot of riders, those who had gotten this far, into a bottleneck. The field narrowed, there was a high gate, it made more sense to take turns going through the gate than to jump the fence at this narrow point. I trotted up to them, still hanging back— Jim West had long since gone through the gate and disappeared—in time to see Brownie Lupton trying to take the fence while behind her, Charlie Madden on Yankee Peddler was demanding that the girl and her big chestnut get out of his way.

"You'll regret this!" yelled Charlie in his booming voice, trying to hold the Peddler, a tall, black, emaciated stallion whose mouth was such—twisted open, upper teeth exposed—that he always appeared to be laughing. Charlie was welcome on any hunt but not the Peddler, an animal known to be eccentric and sometimes dangerous, and whose reactions to mares, even those not in heat, were always unpredictable, often violent.

"Make way!" yelled Charlie, yanking the Peddler to the side while I sat and watched and sensible riders crowded each other through the gate.

The chestnut refused, Brownie nearly taking a toss over the majestic head and ominous fence, then refused again. Finally, all eyes on the imprudent girl and lunging horse, she pulled aside for Charlie.

She pouted, Charlie gave her a scornful glance, then drew back, gathered in the Peddler, and, perched high on the black horse's prominent withers, charged the fence.

Poor Charlie.

Heads turned, the last rider, myself excepted, passed through the gate. Brownie sat wantonly on Polly, who could not stand still, and with sensual silence egged Charlie on. And on he went—too fast, I thought in alarm, too fast.

The Peddler refused. At the last moment he jammed his long black legs straight out in front of him and stopped and, in a movement too fast to see, swerved away from the fence and toward the fiery chestnut, whose scent had just stung his nostrils. Charlie managed to stay on, though he was thrown forward onto the black's long neck, and Brownie, openly scoffing at the little man, held her ground.

Charlie glared at her and, having got himself back in the saddle and hauling the black away from the kicking chestnut just in time, had another try at the fence. Again the black refused and Charlie, flung about like a small child, stayed on.

The third attempt, the third refusal!

Then flushed, eyes as wild as the Peddler's, Charlie pulled the black around once more and applied the whip and drove his spurs into the tender flanks. The black bolted toward the fence.

"Charlie!" I tried to call out, but too late.

There was a crack—was it wood? was it bone? The rails splintered and the Peddler, without a thought of jumping, crashed head-on through the fence. Charlie cursed, on the other side of the fence the Peddler stopped short and flung Charlie straight to the ground. The big horse was stunned yet still on his legs. He shuddered, the body sagged, the head drooped, the long legs were splayed in at the knees and out at the hooves. He looked as if he would never move again. As for Charlie, up he sat, face as red as his pink coat, then—seventy years old! I thought—hopped to his feet and shook his fist at the Peddler.

Any other horse but Yankee Peddler would have fallen immediately to the ground and stayed there. Any other rider but Charlie Madden would have lain on his face where he had landed and not moved. But they weren't injured, either one of them, and the Peddler was still shuddering and Charlie still shaking his fist.

"I would have been all right," exclaimed Brownie Lupton, speaking to me but in a voice loud enough for Charlie to hear, "if that old man hadn't interfered!"

And smiling as falsely as any young girl possibly could, she wheeled Polly about and, avoiding the hole in the fence, splintered and gaping, sailed up and over and down and, with a lively smirk at Charlie, galloped off and out of sight.

"Leg up! Leg up!" cried Charlie.

I rode through the open gate, dismounted, and, seizing in both hands the upraised shin, frail but unbreakable, helped him back up on the Peddler.

"Did you hear that? Did you?"

He looked down at me from his great height and quivered. "Old," Charlie said in a whisper. "Old!"

I nodded.

Again the whip, again the spurs, and the Peddler ceased his shuddering, raised his head, looked wildly about him, and sped away.

I remounted and shut the gate. Then trotted off toward where the hunt must be.

In and out of a gaunt wood, across a frozen brook and icebound fields crusted here and there with patches of powdery snow, on I rode as the light turned a milkier gray and then darkened to black. I heard Jim West's horn, it was getting colder. The countryside rolled and fell away, sky and earth indistinguishable. In the shelter of an abandoned corn-crib I came upon the solitary figure of the portly man. His horse was breathing hard, he himself was smoking a cigarette and taking long drinks from a silver flask.

"Haven't seen you," he said, holding out the flask, which I declined. "No spills I hope?"

"No spills," I said.

"Well then, do you know where we are?"

"I wish I did."

"There's a road back there, I've been on it twice. First time, I met that girl who rode a little way with Welles and me when we started out. She says the problem's that they've let loose the second fox. The first fox and the second, you see, are crossing paths. Going in two circles. Half the hounds on one, half on the other."

"I don't know how West allowed it to happen," I said, removing my gloves and warming my fingers as the portly man capped his flask and puffed the last of his cigarette.

"As if the weather isn't bad enough," he said. "First ice then mud. And in mud there's always the risk of bowed tendons."

I nodded.

"Well," he said, gathering his hunter and turning, "I'm going home. If I can find the way."

"Good luck!" I called.

A riderless horse passed me at a gallop, two men and a woman were off their mounts and crouching around someone stretched out beside his fallen horse, once Alex and I caught sight of each other—she was three fields over—and she gave me a wave. A ditch, a horse attempting to scramble out of it, and suddenly, far ahead, the undaunted sounding of Jim West's horn.

First fox, I wondered, or the second?

Then I saw landmarks, the Stillby farm, the silo rising up like a lighthouse, and barbed-wire fences and a few cows huddled together.

"Buse!" I said, riding up to her. "What's the matter?"

She was sitting on a rock, her shoulders hunched, and

holding the reins of her little washy chestnut with the glaze on his nose.

"DunGannon," she said, with a glance up at her horse. "His tendon. The reason he couldn't race anymore. Remember?"

I nodded, though I remembered nothing of DunGannon's past.

"It's pulled again, after three years. I'm heartbroken."

"How are you going to get him home?" I asked.

"One of the Stillby children saw me. They're calling for a van. I don't know what I'll do if he stays lame."

Her face was chapped, she was resting her elbows on her spread knees, DunGannon was hanging his head and taking the weight off his right foreleg.

"Buse," I said, "I'll wait with you."

"I'm all right," she said. "Please."

"I'll see you at the house, then," I said.

"You're going back?"

I nodded.

"Good for you," said Buse.

It was only a few miles from the Stillby farm to Steepleton. Yet once more the road led me out of open fields and into woods and onto a narrow, unused trail. There was nothing I could do but follow it. I wondered if Charlie had crashed through any more fences or if he had cornered Brownie Lupton in some cul-de-sac. Martha knew we were headed home, I patted the slender neck, her trot quickened. The trees were close together, blackened as if by fire.

Then Martha shied. She reared, whinnied, and swung her hindquarters off the trail, smashing herself against a tree, and caught off guard and clinging to her neck, I heard the rush of air, saw the flash of color, stared as a small bright red fox—the second fox!—shot from between Martha's front legs and, before I could regain my seat, vanished somewhere just ahead of us. Fox! I thought, more startled than the ordinarily well-behaved Martha. But no sooner had I begun to calm the little mare than half a dozen hounds were swarming upon us, rushing between and around Martha's dancing legs, rolling their tongues, setting up a din louder than the brassy hymns we had heard at the start of the day. I tried to hold Martha, I tried to make way for the bitches.

Martha bolted.

My docile mare could stand no more. Fox and hounds appearing without warning and with no regard for horse and horseman were enough to throw any horse into a panic, and Martha had given way to panic.

Fox in the lead, hounds in pursuit, Martha running away, brighter light ahead—at least we were nearing the edge of the interminable wood—and behind us another horse. Gaining. I wanted to deny the sounds of it, the speechless thundering of the approaching hooves, wanted to deny that there could possibly be another runaway horse on this trail too narrow even for my own slight mare. But behind us the living locomotive was almost upon us and would not pull up, slow down, make any attempt to avoid us. Martha spurted ahead, fell back. No use. Accident, I thought, and a bad one.

Daylight, fading or not, and open space, safety, exactly at the moment when the other horse overtook us and was suddenly halfway across the cemetery. Private property was one thing, I thought, cemetery another. Then I knew where I was, took it all in.

Brownie Lupton. The Van Fleet family cemetery. The hounds. The fox. No way to stop.

The hounds were dodging the tombstones, as was I, brown and white bitches after blood and cascading through the cemetery and around Walter T. Van Fleet's mausoleum—there it stood, horseshoe wreath long withered away, glass and marble, columns and massive door blackened in shadow, sheathed in ice—while Brownie, who had lost her black cap, drove Pretty Polly straight toward the mausoleum. Brownie turned and, recognizing me, gave a wave, then jumped it. The oddly white-faced girl, the chestnut as reckless as she was, the two of them sailing above old Walter's last resting place—suddenly I thought of a phantom Hal sitting beside me on Marcabru.

Barely avoiding a small discolored angel with downcast

face and a chipped wing, I thought of Alex, and glanced down. Martha, I saw—I had tired her at last, riding around the rim of the cemetery—was standing with her right front hoof well beyond the edge of a new and as yet unmarked grave. With the pressure of my right calf and still looking down, quickly I moved her off.

No headstone yet.

That night, I thought, this was one anecdote that would not be told.

Why was the place so silent? Where were they?

I had taken so much time to reach Steepleton, crossing the macadam road that fronted the way into the cemetery and entering a growth of new alders on the other side, letting Martha guide us home until unerringly she brought us out into the lower meadow, that I assumed they would all be back, voices loud and spirits high at the end of the first day's hunt. I thought of Jim West praising one of the bitches and of the shy hound staring up at Jim with the helpless look of devotion peculiar to foxhounds. And thought of Alex consoling Buse for DunGannon's leg. And of Charlie edging through the crowd toward Brownie Lupton too tired for flight. No serious accidents, no badly broken bones.

But it was not so. None of it.

I rugged up Martha, a boy I didn't know appeared with her gruel. There wasn't another horse in the stable, except Marcabru. I detoured toward his stall, turned back.

I entered the house through the kitchen and was immediately in the way of the hired chef and his staff, so passed quickly into the dining room, where the buffet was in preparation—long table pushed against the wall beneath the painting of the young wife smiling in her sleep—and heard the unpleasant silence of the great house that was emptier, despite the men in the kitchen, than the stable.

What was wrong?

A wisp of smoke, the sound of a log disintegrating into hot coals in the fireplace, a moment's speculation about

Brownie Lupton—something, whatever it was, drew me into the darkened salon, where at once I saw not Brownie Lupton but Charlie Madden. In shadows above the fireplace the painting of two foxhounds and a rising pheasant, no light at the leaded panes of glass in the tall windows, silence except for the sound of another log—and the person I'd least expected to see.

"Charlie?" I started to say, and got no farther.

Head on a cushion, booted left leg dangling toward the floor, pink coat ripped open, there he lay on the divan beneath the portrait of Whistlejacket. His face was gray, his eyes were closed, the mouth hung slack. He looked as if two or three of our party had merely dumped him in that improbable place and gone off.

I stepped closer, pulled a spindly chair to the divan, and, perched on the edge of the seat, peered down at Charlie.

I whispered his name, leaned closer. As far as I could see, he had stopped breathing. I spoke his name. Behind me the fire, burning low on the andirons fit for some royal hunting lodge, sent a glow into the failing light.

Suddenly Charlie's eyelids opened, narrowed—I startled despite myself—and the hard little eyes glared up at me.

"Charlie," I whispered. "It's Mike."

He watched me, his body inert, his eyes bright with suspicion.

"They've given me up," he said, the familiar deep voice sinking back down inside him as soon as he spoke. I leaned closer, must have frowned in puzzlement.

"For dead!" came the voice broken but impatient. "For dead! What do you think?"

"Charlie," I said, trying to hide my shock and keep my voice soft, "they've just gone for help."

"Speak up, can't you?"

"It's better if you don't talk," I said.

"If you have to stay," he said, his chin trembling, "keep quiet! Let an old man die in peace."

"You're not—" I started to say, then caught myself. His voice was stronger, and there was no disobeying the little blazing eyes. Charlie to the last, I thought.

"Did I ever tell you," he said abruptly, "about the fox we couldn't catch until he took cover in a neighbor's barn?"

"Please," I said.

"If it hadn't been for me," he said, wandering, "no one would have known what happened to those three leading hounds. Fox jumped down a well—I saw him—and the hounds jumped right in after him. Thanks to me, we fished them out. Fox half dead when we hauled them up. Hounds finished the job on the spot . . ."

I smiled in spite of myself, shook my head.

"Jim West was pulling your leg," he said after a pause, glaring up at me and narrowing his lids, whether accusing me or amusing himself, I couldn't tell. "And you believed him!"

"I believe you, Charlie," I said quietly.

"Mistake," he said. His eyes closed, flew open again.

"I liked that girl," he said suddenly. "Nice girl . . ."

He paused, there was not a sound. The fire shifted, far off in the kitchen a platter fell and smashed.

"Hope she's all right," he said. "We gave her quite a jolt!"

Then he stopped, changed again to the Charlie he wanted me to remember.

"Followed her, caught her! Left it all to the Peddler, didn't have to do a thing except stay on. Never saw so many fences. Posts and rails, stone walls as high as you find in Ireland. Regular steeplechase. Kept her in sight, though, found her easy enough. Kept gaining . . ."

"Charlie," I said, leaning forward, squeezing his shoulder, "tell me later. . . ."

"Now," he said, "or never!"

"I'm listening," I said quickly.

"Bet you are. But you argue. You interrupt."

I waited.

"Worst accident I've ever seen. Ever. She was close. Suddenly close. Looked as if she was standing still and I didn't bother to ask myself why. Forgot all about the Peddler. Too busy thinking about the quarry. Well, the Peddler went up on his hind legs and hit the mare—"

"Charlie," I said, giving him a shake.

"Leave me alone, can't you?"

He sulked. Then he began to grin.

"Peddler went up on his hind legs and hit the mare—it never occurred to me he'd be up to his old tricks and try to mount that mare—but up he went, we struck with a jolt no matter how I pulled and sawed on his mouth and yelled at him. If the mare had been a hand or two shorter, the Peddler would have toppled horse and girl right there. But the mare was big, high and solid in the rear, so despite the Peddler's head hanging over the girl's shoulder and the poor girl suddenly tangled up in the hooves and front legs of a frantic stallion, the mare didn't fall and the Peddler didn't unseat the girl. But she looked around at me, more angry than frightened or startled, and never in my life have I felt so foolish. How do you apologize when your stallion's mounted a young girl's mare while the girl's still on her? But the situation was worse than that.

"The problem was that the girl had stopped at the edge of a slope, a steep one and a long way down, one you couldn't descend except slowly, with care. And as soon as the Peddler hit the mare he knocked her over the edge, girl and all. One look full in my face from the girl, one scream of indignation from the mare, and down they went, and the Peddler and I with them. The mare shot out from under the Peddler, the Peddler dropped, trumpeting once in pain and surprise— how could the poor beast understand such injustice?—and somehow the two animals kept their footing while the girl and I stayed on. I'm sure the Peddler thought that if only he could reach the bottom of that endless slope still on his feet, he'd be able to mount his mare in peace. But both horses descended fast, and just as we got to level ground, the Peddler fell. I swerved him—at least I did that much—and went down with the Peddler. I saw the girl, I saw her cap— she had lost it on landing—I saw her black, hard cap flying around under the hooves of the mare. Soccer, I thought, as the mare kicked along the cap, soccer! Then I hit.

"If you believe all that," whispered Charlie without a pause and giving me a crooked smile, "you're more gullible than I thought. But it's true."

The sound of a car's wheels, the sound of splintering ice.

Voices outside, greetings, then inside heavy footsteps on parquet floors. Approaching. No hurry. Charlie opened his eyes, looked up at me, the crooked smile becoming a grimace of scorn.

"Fox hunters," he said, as they entered the grand salon, "foxes. The unspeakable in full pursuit of the uneatable."

"Wilde," I nearly said, but kept quiet.

"Oscar Wilde," said Charlie, spared the sight of those who had come for him.

14

"ILL-FATED," ALEX said under her breath. Nothing more. She passed me—they had already carried Charlie out—and went up to her rooms. The word spread, hot water began running in hidden tubs and showers. Someone tossed several logs on the fire. Alex had planned a fortepiano recital for the evening of the third day of the hunt, but now it was canceled, as was the rest of the hunt.

I was not tempted to try Alex's connecting door and left my own as it was. Bolted. I lay soaking in the deep tub. Aimless. The gravel path, I thought for no apparent reason, stops abruptly, the path of sand makes a circle, the brick path is without end. Which one should I take? Pointless thinking. Why now? Then it came to me—the highway, Carol, dinner instead of lunch at The Flying Crane. Tomorrow night. The night after.

Heavy corduroys, a checked flannel shirt, the heaviest tweed jacket I own. Then the Minox, which I've kept under some handkerchiefs in the small drawer of my bureau since moving into Hal's rooms. It is a camera made for concealing in the palm of the hand, which is to say for secrecy. I hardly expected to discover secrets among people who had been the context of Charlie Madden's death and who were only waiting for the next morning, when they could leave. Still I was in a mood for secrecy. Mine. So I put the Minox in the pocket of my tweed jacket.

The sound of doors closing, voices coming up from below. Ice in glasses. Charlie had been given old Walter's suite, which made me think of the word "rotation." A nice word. Virgie in the room once designated for the oldest child, Brownie Lupton spending another night in Virgie's former bed. Or was she in the smaller room with the two daybeds?

I saw Buse coming down the hall and met her at the top of the stairs. Now of all times she wasn't drinking. Buse in jeans and a loose black fisherman's sweater. She was going to the stable. DunGannon's leg was a good excuse, she said. I understood and felt a new liking for Buse, whose breath smelled as clear as a spring. I joined her out the back way and to the stable.

"We can't come in here," I said, "without Harry knowing."

"Harry doesn't care about DunGannon or me or you either," she said, opening the stall door and making a sound of commiseration, in the darkness bending and running her hand gently down DunGannon's leg.

"Poor boy," she said. "This time I think we're through."

She stood up, leaned against the horse's shoulder, sighed. The lithe chestnut was so swaddled in blankets from head to croup that he resembled a medieval horse waiting for armor. A long wait, I thought.

"I'm going to have to sell him," said Buse, "though I won't know for sure until tomorrow. Look at him, he knows what I'm talking about. Don't you, boy?"

Some of the transient horses were stabled in the corridors between the rows of box stalls, saddles had been dumped everywhere, bales of hay had been broken open in front of the stalls. Now and then the face of an unfamiliar horse poked over a partition. Too many guests, too many horses, too little time. Chaos in Alex's stable, a sleepless night for Harry.

"I don't want to go back up there," Buse said in the shadows, "do you?"

I waited.

"I'll be all right in a while. But today—it's just too close to Hal."

I brought a couple of horse blankets, we heaped up a pile of straw, left DunGannon's stall door ajar. We half sat, half lay beneath the blankets.

"Horses smell different at night than in the daytime," said Buse.

I nodded. Already we were warming each other. And now, I thought, or in a minute, she'll talk about Hal, as of course she did.

"I love him," she said as a nearby horse kicked in its sleep, snorted. "I've never stopped loving him. I didn't care that Alex came first or that Alex took precedence every time or that no matter how long I lived with them there was nothing I could expect from Hal except the privilege, as he said, of sharing his bed. I still want that privilege. He said he'd never hurt me, never abandon me, never send me back to Peter. Peter's my husband. I left him practically after the honeymoon for Hal. He's still waiting."

Then, twisting a little in my direction, "Wouldn't it be funny if Alex has told you all this already?" she said. "You'd stop me, wouldn't you? I'd hate to talk on like the goose Hal said I was."

For answer I worked my arm around her shoulder, squeezed, relaxed, squeezed. I felt her reassurance in the way she let herself go against me.

"I can't help it," she said, more to herself than me. "I miss him and I want that privilege. He said it was the one thing I could count on. He said that satyriasis ran in the family, though he laughed at the word. He said no matter what happened he wouldn't fail me. Toward the end—how could we know it was coming?—he told me his marriage was going to change, that he wanted to treat Alex like the wife she'd been to him all along. Things would change, they'd be alone more often. Sometimes they might eat alone. And they'd go on trips. But he'd always return, he said, and I'd share his bed as often as I always had and that, he said, ought to be enough."

She paused. Shifted in the hay. Then, her face closer to mine, her voice softer, she continued.

"Alex found him. But I was with him the night before he died. Think of it. Our last night together. What now? No man could return to a woman again and again for all those years and not love her. Hal always said sex was love and I believe him."

She paused, rested her head on my shoulder.

"Interesting theory," I said, wondering if Yankee Peddler was somewhere in the stable, "but didn't you ever feel humiliation?"

"Never," she said, quick to answer. "Alex once said she hated him, but I knew she didn't. There were other women—girls really—and we did things that must have been hard on Alex. Not on me, though, once I got used to what we were doing. And I was especially fond of one of the young women. She was her own person. That's what she said. Small. Lots of spunk."

Parachutes, I thought, and smiled.

"My name's Barbara," she said then. "Did you know that?"

"I think so," I said.

"I never understood why Hal didn't like it," she said, "but he didn't. Alexandra was a splendid name, he said, that left Barbara flat. I don't remember when he raised this matter of names, only that we were in the beginning of summer and that I hadn't lived with them long. The stall and stable doors were open, I was cleaning the hooves of Toots's pony—she wouldn't groom that pony, not Toots—and every now and then Hal leaned down and while I was helpless, stooped over as I was and holding the pony's leg and picking away at the hoof, he stroked my bottom. That was the afternoon he nicknamed me Buse. He had never liked my husband, he said again, and he said a woman who was as much woman as me deserved a man's name, especially the name of that husband of mine. Technically Peter and I were married. That's all. Sometimes I wondered if Hal didn't decide to call me Buse just to remind himself of what he'd done to Peter."

"I like Barbara more than Buse," I said.

"Doesn't do me much good now," she said. "Too late to change. Besides, he wanted a Buse, I'm a Buse. He used lots of rhymes that afternoon—"

"Like *bustier*," I said, interrupting.

"Sure," she said, "that sounds right. Anyway, he kept joking and stroked my bottom while I worked on his daughter's pony, and then, giving me a slap on my seat, he said I was a goose and walked off."

She shivered, my right arm was around her shoulder, she raised her right hand and took hold of mine. I drew the blankets higher. Far down the cobblestoned aisle a horse was drinking.

"You know," Buse said with a giggle, "anyone seeing us now would jump to conclusions."

"The wrong ones," I said laughing, "but justified."

She shifted again, I could feel her looking up into the darkness. Then once more she surprised me.

"Funny," she said, "I love Alex. I loved her from the beginning. Sometimes I'm not sure the feeling's reciprocal. But I always knew I was in that house thanks to her. And I always admired her. There aren't many wives who'll share their husbands, anyway not in the kind of marriage Hal and Alex had. She's a generous woman. Of course there wasn't any question—she was the wife, not me. I never envied her except when I wished I'd met Hal first, and that's normal. But I suppose he wouldn't have married me if I had. I'm not an accomplished woman. I remember a night when Hal and I were waiting for Alex to come down and play one of her pieces on the fortepiano. I always wondered why it wasn't pianoforte. But that's just me."

Another shiver and suddenly I knew she wanted me to hold both her hands. The incident she was recalling didn't seem to warrant the strength of her grip.

"Hal turned on the lamp, got out some sheets of music. Then Alex came in and there were just the three of us. She was wearing a special gown, a gift from Hal. It was dark beige trimmed with silver sequins and some sort of black material. The gown itself was of lambskin. Split lambskin. Well, she entered the room, Hal took a step toward her, she turned around. She was wearing the dress for the first time and I'd never seen anything like it, nor had Hal. The gown was open in back, the two sides of the dress went up to her shoulders like narrow wings—they actually had layers of short feathers on them, made of the black material. There was a strap high up that held the wings together, and those wings were just far enough apart to show about an inch of Alex's left shoulder blade and above the hips were so wide I wanted to put my hand in there and onto her bare flesh. There was a zipper on the wings and it was open all the way to the bottom of her spine. No wonder Hal stepped forward. But Alex had twisted when she had turned her back to us, and long ridges swept down to where the hem of the skirt lay on the floor in a circle about five feet in diameter. I've never seen any dress so tight, the rest of the zipper—closed—followed the crease of the buttocks all the way, otherwise she couldn't have put on the dress. But everything made us look at Alex's bottom. The wings narrowed to a point along the closed zipper, the lambskin was as thin as a fingernail around her buttocks and tight, there were highlights. And that was a time when Alex was wearing her hair longer and on this evening she had put it up in a French braid, which is a way of fixing the hair from the scalp outwards, so the braid starts high on the head and follows the center of the head to the base of the neck. She had put on pearl earrings. There I sat in my cardigan and wool dress, legs crossed, and there stood Alex, the lower half of her, especially the rounded part, looking like a piece of polished wood. Yet that body wasn't made of wood.

"In another step Hal was at her side. As clearly as anything I've ever seen I saw his beautiful thumb and first finger pull the zipper the rest of the way down so that I saw her shiny buttocks. I knew I'd never have buttocks like that. Then his hand was on her bare waist, the gown hung open, and without a thought of me or the music he steered her out of the room."

"And still," I said immediately, wishing I had held my tongue, "still you didn't feel envy."

She said nothing, which convinced me she had not heard my comment, but instead she gave a shudder that I could feel down her entire length.

"Buse," I said, but she was shuddering against me and clenching my hands in hers. Shuddering for Hal, I thought, and I hung on as poor Buse shuddered without a sound. I had felt nothing like it, ever, and wished it would end. She was strong, her hands were slippery, for a moment it appeared that she might break free. But I held her.

Finally it subsided, she went limp, I cradled her as best I could. We waited.

"And," she said, a touch of humor back in her voice, "and you couldn't even give me a kiss."

It was about 2:00 A.M. when we reached the house, hurrying against the cold, Buse draped in one of the horse blankets, I holding her arm and clutching the upturned collar of my jacket. We stole in quietly yet needn't have, since even before we entered the darkened dining room—no remnants of the buffet—we heard the sounds of the forte-piano. The door to the grand salon was closed, perhaps out of thoughtfulness for her sleeping guests. But we paused together and listened.

"It's what she was going to play in the recital," said Buse.

"Mozart," I murmured.

"Whatever," she said.

"Let's go in," I whispered.

"Not me," she said, "I'm going up."

I followed her, and at the top of the stairway we faced each other, kissed. Then we went to our rooms.

I remembered the camera. Too late.

"They're gone," Virgie said. "Wake up!"

She gave me a shake, I smiled without opening my eyes. Morning, I wondered, or night? A small hand on my shoulder, a rough shake.

"I want you to wake up, Mike," she said.

"Virgie," I said, looking at her, rolling over, "what are you doing in here?"

I might have understood if Alex had appeared in my room and in fact I'd been half expecting her, if not in the last darkness then now when the sun, as I saw at my window, was high. Alex yes, but Virgie?

"Come along," she said, and gave my arm a tug.

"Listen," I said, sitting up, "what's the matter?"

"Nothing," she said, "just get up."

I started to reach toward the foot of the bed and my robe, but she was quicker. The robe fell across my lap. I swung my feet over the edge.

"Where—" I began, then stopped, seeing her face. Something, I thought, was wrong with her.

"My room," she said, and waited.

"Ah," I said, "Brownie," and struggled into the robe.

"Not funny," she said. Then, changing her tone, "But it's curious. Did you hear Mother playing last night?"

I nodded.

"Well, Brownie and I were in there first. On the divan."

"I see."

"Enough," she said.

"Where's Alex?"

"In bed. She had breakfast in bed."

"Maybe I'll just say good morning. . . ."

"Look," she said, "I told you. My room."

"So Brownie's gone," I said.

Her lips tightened. She was wearing jeans, a sweatshirt, jodhpur boots.

"Let's go," she said.

Open doors, silence, empty rooms, towels on floors and beds. I knew that down below the trucks and vans were gone, as Virgie had said. And Charlie's white monster? At least someone else, not I, could worry about that abandoned antiquated car and the new horse trailer hitched to its rear.

"I'd like to get dressed, Virgie," I said, even as she closed and locked her door behind us and turned and pulled off the sweatshirt. The shades and drapes were drawn, the bed unmade. The jeans were snug on her little hips, the torso white. I hadn't expected the size of the breasts.

"Recognize the room?"

"As a matter of fact I don't."

"My sister's. Daddy found her in that closet."

She made a gesture with her chin. I refused to look. Holding a bedpost, she removed first one boot then the other. Black stockings and jeans. Like Alex.

"Virgie," I said, "must we do this?"

"Yes. While Mother's in bed with her newspaper."

"Why?"

"It's what I want, Mike. I'll tell you what to do. You listen. Do what I tell you to do. If you think you're humoring me, you're wrong."

The room darkened though outside the cold sun was climbing toward noon. Virgie, still holding the bedpost with one hand then the other, pulled at the jeans, stepped out of them. Black stockings, no garter belt. What had she worn in the grand salon with Brownie? Nylon pajamas? She turned and scrambled onto the bed, propped her back against the headboard, spread her legs.

"Out of the robe," she said, "and the pajama bottoms."

"That's all?"

"And come over here."

At least there was the flannel top, I thought, and attempted to join her.

"Not like that!" she cried. "Not on all fours! The lotus position, hands on knees!"

I remembered the cover of a book, a young woman in a white leotard, and sat cross-legged at Virgie's upturned feet in a position intended for contemplation, surely, nothing else.

"Better," she said. "The idea is to look like a Buddha."

"I'm too thin—" I started to say.

"Ready?"

I wasn't, but I nodded, in the unnatural light faced Virgie, who was sitting upright, spread legs extended, and wearing nothing but black stockings.

"Now," she said, "slide off one of the stockings. Your choice."

I reached forward before I realized that I would have to move closer, sit between Virgie's legs and not at her feet if I were to reach the top of one of the stockings and close my hands around her thigh.

"God," she said, "you're ungainly!"

Again in position, hands on knees, back straight, pajama top sparing me full embarrassment. I leaned forward and with curved palms and fingers seized her and began to draw down the stocking on her left leg. It slid, it rolled, it gathered, I stirred, deftly I worked the stocking over the foot and free of the toes.

"Here," she said, less sternly and reaching out her hand.

Eyes on me, the large eyes that were a match for the teeth, she held the top of the stocking in one hand, the toe in the other, and slowly drew its length back and forth under her nose. Then stopped, returned the black formless silk to me.

I followed suit, waited.

"What do you smell? Nothing?"

I nodded.

"Now ball it up and stuff it between my legs—do I have to tell you?—and try it again. Same way."

"Virgie," I exclaimed, "please . . ."

"Do it, Mike," she said. "You'll be surprised."

Stocking crumpled between Virgie's thighs. Rotating motions. Gently. Her eyes were closed.

Then, slowly, I sniffed the entire length of the stocking. Again. Again. Her breasts rising and falling.

"Well?"

For answer I dropped the stocking, abandoned my silly lotus position, pulled her down. At last. We embraced and to the end I kept glancing first to the white thigh on my left, then to its black twin on my right. Half a little French maid.

"Now," she said, pushing me off, "go to Mother."

I lay on my back on Alex's wide bed. In only her jacquard dressing gown, she sat on the plush bench in front of her mirror. Suddenly I had a thought.

"Alex," I said, without lowering my eyes or turning to look at her, "who do you really love, Hal or Harry?"

She waited, smiled into the glass.

"You," she said.

CODA—CAROL

"YOU LOOK LIKE the cat who ate the mouse."

"You're right. It was one of those things of a lifetime."

"Tell me."

"This morning. Dawn coming up after a night of snow turned to rain. I was returning from one of those walks I love to take, admiring the sun on the desolation of that time of day. Not a person in sight. Walls and fire escapes creeping out of darkness. Glistening. It so happened that the wet streets were lined with refuse—sacks, tin cans too full for their lids, bundles tied up but bursting their bonds, old umbrellas.

"I heard a car behind me. Only one. It passed, then about a block ahead of me pulled over and stopped. I slowed my pace. The driver got out, a young man dressed for an office and carrying a briefcase. He looked up and down the street. Quickly. No one in sight. Except for me and apparently I didn't count. Then quickly he crossed over to one of the more conspicuous mountains of trash and junk, looked around him, took something from the briefcase and pushed it into a tilting can. Then back to his car and away."

"A furtive fellow."

"Yes."

"Something to hide. Guilty."

"Yes. But my intuition had been aroused. He had looked at me for a moment before getting into the car. I had seen him, but would I go poking into old trash cans? He really had no alternative but to decide he was safe and drive off."

"Safe? From you? That's a funny idea!"

"Oh, well, I guess you don't want to hear what happened."

"Tell me. Only I know already what happened."

"We'll see about that."

"If you hurry."

"You're right. I investigated."

"Hmmm."

"A whole street of curtained windows, faces behind them for all I knew, someone getting ready to emerge from a basement apartment with a dog. Into the cold."

"A big boxer."

"A Doberman."

"And catch you with the goods. Really, you're no better than the man in the car."

"But what did I find?"

"Something that caused the man all that guilt."

"Well?"

"Oh, a gun. Or a packet of letters. Papers from his office."

"You may know what happened, but you don't know what I found. Ready? I crossed the street as quickly as he had. Stopped at the same can. And found it. Just as I thought. Jammed down into the can. A magazine. With a green cover. Undamaged."

"You mean to say you retrieved it?"

"What else?"

"You really cared what that poor man was trying to get rid of?"

"It was my intuition, you see. I had to know if it was right. So just as hastily as the man had disposed of his magazine, or tried to, I saved it from some public dump and oblivion."

"You couldn't just leave it alone."

"Not at all. It wasn't my magazine, I hadn't put it there. Yet when I saw it and pulled it from the can, I hoped no one was looking."

"Catching, huh?"

"I rolled it up, crossed back to my side of the street, walked home more rapidly than usual."

"What kind of magazine?"

"English."

"And?"

"I'm sure you know."

"One of those."

"Exactly. Soft as soap. A couple of sweet young things on a beach. Bums and peaches. Ads. Home photos. Printing smeared, out of alignment."

"So you're pleased with yourself."

"Immensely. Think of the incongruity. The tricks of chance. The reliability of a hunch. The evidence you can't destroy. The fact that he'd have such a magazine in the first place and then be trying to get rid of it. You have to admit it's unusual."

"Oh, come on. You just like the blondes on the beach."

"Shall we look?"

ABOUT THE AUTHOR

John Hawkes is the distinguished author of many works of fiction, among them *The Blood Oranges*, *The Lime Twig*, and *Adventures in the Alaskan Skin Trade*. He is a member of the American Academy and Institute of Arts and Letters and the American Academy of Arts and Sciences. Mr. Hawkes teaches at Brown University.

Ballard, J. G. *The Day of Creation.*	ISBN 0-02-041514-1
Beattie, Ann. *Where You'll Find Me.*	ISBN 0-02-016560-9
Cantor, Jay. *Krazy Kat.*	ISBN 0-02-042081-1
Carrère, Emmanuel. *The Mustache.*	ISBN 0-02-018870-6
Coover, Robert. *A Night at the Movies.*	ISBN 0-02-019120-0
Coover, Robert. *Whatever Happened to Gloomy Gus of the Chicago Bears?*	ISBN 0-02-042781-6
Dickinson, Charles. *With or Without.*	ISBN 0-02-019560-5
Handke, Peter. *Across.*	ISBN 0-02-051540-5
Handke, Peter. *Repetition.*	ISBN 0-02-020762-X
Handke, Peter. *Slow Homecoming.*	ISBN 0-02-051530-8
Handke, Peter. *3 X Handke.*	ISBN 0-02-020761-1
Havazelet, Ehud. *What Is It Then Between Us?*	ISBN 0-02-051750-5
Hawkes, John. *Whistlejacket.*	ISBN 0-02-043591-6
Hemingway, Ernest. *The Garden of Eden.*	ISBN 0-684-18871-6
Mathews, Harry. *Cigarettes.*	ISBN 0-02-013971-3
Miller, John (Ed.). *Hot Type.*	ISBN 0-02-044701-9
Morrow, Bradford. *Come Sunday.*	ISBN 0-02-023001-X
Olson, Toby. *The Woman Who Escaped from Shame.*	ISBN 0-02-023231-4
Olson, Toby. *Utah.*	ISBN 0-02-098410-3
Pelletier, Cathie. *The Funeral Makers.*	ISBN 0-02-023610-7
Phillips, Caryl. *A State of Independence.*	ISBN 0-02-015080-6
Pritchard, Melissa. *Spirit Seizures.*	ISBN 0-02-036070-3
Rush, Norman. *Whites.*	ISBN 0-02-023841-X
Tallent, Elizabeth. *Time with Children.*	ISBN 0-02-045540-2
Theroux, Alexander. *An Adultery.*	ISBN 0-02-008821-3
Vargas Llosa, Mario. *Who Killed Palomino Molero?*	ISBN 0-02-022570-9
West, Paul. *Rat Man of Paris.*	ISBN 0-02-026250-7

*Available from your local bookstore, or from Macmillan Publishing Company,
100K Brown Street, Riverside, New Jersey 08370*